CW00833219

A Path for Serpents

Paul Harris, long-time Far Eastern business-man, is back in Malaysia after years of living in France. The jungle is about the only thing he recognizes; everything else is subject to change, skyscrapers replacing sprawling colonial buildings, traffic hysterical, and the old tempo of easy living replaced by executive stress.

Almost from the moment of Paul's arrival in Kuala Lumpur, what had seemed in France not much more than a mercy mission becomes something very different. A minor local difficulty turns quickly into big trouble leading to murder, then sees Paul on the run in a country that had once been home to him, but now rejects him.

He flees to Thailand, but the killers follow, and it takes one of the most hair-raising journeys of his life, plus a little fast footwork and a lot of luck, before he is safely back in France with mission accomplished.

GAVIN BLACK

A Path for Serpents

THE CRIME CLUB
An Imprint of HarperCollins *Publishers*

First published in Great Britain in 1991
by The Crime Club, an imprint of
HarperCollins Publishers, 77–85 Fulham Palace Road,
Hammersmith, London W6 8JB

A catalogue record for this book is
available from the British Library

ISBN 0 00 232355 9

Photoset in Linotron Baskerville by
Rowland Phototypesetting Ltd
Bury St Edmunds, Suffolk
Printed and bound in Great Britain by
HarperCollins Book Manufacturing, Glasgow

CHAPTER 1

The double gates of the jail looked as though they hadn't been opened wide for years, all the human traffic in and out through a small hatch. There was a doorbell and I rang it. From inside came a suburban buzzing. After a second ring the hatch opened. A Malay in khaki shirt and shorts put his head out. My skin colour, pale from a French winter, made him use English.

'What want?'

I said in Malay: 'I have a permit to see a prisoner.'

The document was on blue paper, the colour making it seem important. The Malay took it. The hatch shut.

I turned to watch the road. Heat shimmering off black asphalt was almost strong enough to produce a couple of mirages. A taxi came past with all the glass closed to keep in the air-conditioning, but still leaking Chinese pop from a radio turned up full. Coming the other way was a lorry loaded with the white vegetable root which, eaten uncooked, can cause death with convulsions. The only pedestrian was a Malay woman swaying towards me on clicking wooden sandals. On one arm she had at least half a dozen bangles, all gold. Her pink blouse showed sweat stains. She didn't bother to pull a portion of her head covering over her face as a defence against the eyes of a lusting foreigner. I was investigated by one longish look, then dismissed as yet another European come to visit a relation on schedule to be hanged for drug-smuggling. She moved away, buttocks saying she was getting fat, and liked it.

In shade I was sweating, too. I heard the hatch open and turned. The warder used his own language.

'You can come in.'

He was not one of the handsome Malays, on the short side, and the good life looking after prisoners had put considerable excess weight down his frontage. Also, his father, or perhaps his grandfather, had told him all about the horrors of British rule and he kept that data constantly recallable. He didn't like having to look up at me.

Beyond the hatch I had been expecting a cement-held, echoing coolness, but it wasn't like that, just more raw sunlight and a courtyard to cross. Ahead was a solid two-storey block with a walkway through it to another courtyard. We were on concrete, the warder's boots drowning out the furtive hissing of my shoes.

We went into shade. The warder pointed to an open door, then exercised his English.

'There. Wait!'

You do a lot of that in the Far East these days. I went into a place about twelve feet square with an unglazed, barred window, a table and two chairs. The table was rough deal and looked as though some part of a punishment routine was scrubbing the top with a hard brush for a couple of hours. The room's décor was dark green paint, the bullying of this slightly eased by a large, white wallposter featuring numbered instructions in English, Malay, and Chinese, a conduct guide for evildoers during their brief contacts with visitors from the outside world.

I took the chair which gave me a view out into the corridor. Sitting there, I had the thought that I should have been searched. I might have been carrying an outsize file, or a revolver, or hashish for a prisoner syndicate.

I looked at my watch. It was twenty past noon. When I looked at it again it was ten to one. During that time no one had come near me. Passing warders had glanced in, but that was all. I heard voices, and doors banging, and noises I couldn't identify. The almost aggressive anger I had brought to this place was being diluted by the waiting.

I hadn't wanted to come back to Malaysia. My life in France seemed to be putting a cover on the old sentimentalities which can be so adhesive in memory. I no longer came half awake at night to remember riding a pony through the pale, misted dawns of Kelantan, or to recall detail of the road which winds up from the steaming heat of Kuala Lumpur to the coolness of the Peak at Frazer's Hill. I didn't think of Kuantan either, where I had kept my boat, but now I was going to see it again. Rumours of big change there had reached me. Instead of the old Resthouse where the dining-room had offered the same salad every night, plus an almost rigidly unchanging menu, there were now two huge tourist hotels facing the South China Sea. Both claimed in advertising to offer displays of native dancing, whatever that might be. These days in Kuala Lumpur you can pay to be frightened by real live headhunters brought over from Borneo.

A warder's boots were noisy, but there was no sound from a prisoner's battered plimsolls. Li Fong Chi was suddenly standing in the doorway with his guard behind him. I nearly stood, then decided against this.

The last time I had seen Li he was twenty-two but looked a lot younger. Now he was twenty-nine and the boy had completely disappeared. In a street I wouldn't have known him. For a moment I had the feeling they had brought me the wrong man. He stood blinking as though long hours in a cell had slowed down his rate of recovery from sun dazzle. If he recognized me he gave no sign.

He might be on drugs, or the victim of rough handling. Li's lawyer, who claimed to have seen the prisoner a number of times, had found his client totally unresponsive. In his office half way up a downtown skyscraper Ming Kai Tek had kept spreading his hands apart in a gesture indicating near-professional despair. I got the message that he wanted away from the case fast, hoping that I would assist his escape by hiring someone with a criminal practice. Family lawyers don't like visiting jails.

Li had not been tidied up for this meeting. That he was unshaven didn't matter on a face that could only have grown a sage's beard, but the stains on his olive-coloured shirt had been there for some time. Prison issue shorts might have been a grubby relic from the Japanese Occupation. Then the military conquerors of Asia had believed that male knees were obscene, and must be covered. Below this modesty Li's legs were bare right down into the plimsolls.

The warder said: 'Go on in!'

Li took two steps forward, hesitated, then shuffled to behind the vacant chair. He didn't pull this back from the table, as though one of the rules he lived under was that you didn't move prison furniture about. The warder leaned against a door jamb, at ease with the world he had made for himself. He issued another order: 'Sit down!'

That was official permission. Li pulled out the chair and sat opposite, settling with his hands in his lap, eyes lowered. It was up to me to make the start in these proceedings, which wasn't easy. I was still trying to find something approaching the right words when Li looked up, but not at me. He was studying those printed rules on the wall to find out whether he was breaking any of them. It seemed he had been. He brought up both hands and put them, palm downwards, on the table. I had to resist a pity that wouldn't serve my purpose.

After years out of the country I didn't trust my Malay or Cantonese, so I used English. The warder was too relaxed to be responsible for any report on this interview, which meant a microphone somewhere. I began by explaining that I had done nothing in the two and a half months since Li's arrest because I had known nothing about it until a phone call from Malaysia to my home in the south of France. The voice had been a woman's, in somewhat uncertain English, and this blurred by the distance it had to travel, possibly from an electric storm over the Burmese mountains. The lady had resisted all interruptions from my end as though she had a piece to say and had to get it all out before she forgot something important. Then, quite suddenly, she ended on a bid for a pathetic appeal: 'Please help me!' I asked if she was Li's wife and I think she said yes, but she rang off before I could put any more questions.

I put my questions to a Kuala Lumpur lawyer I had once used to sell my house in that city and whom I knew had also functioned for the Lis when they were building their Trengannu hôtel. Ming Kai Tek didn't have to consult his files, he had all the facts available for serving and I listened with my defences against any personal involvement starting to crumble.

Li was on remand after being charged. It seemed likely he would have to wait for months before trial, an ordeal that could be aimed at breaking down morale as a means to a 'free' confession. Ming didn't begin to say this over the phone, but I could practically hear the ticking in his mind. Then, and later in his Kuala Lumpur office, the lawyer wore discretion like a bullet-proof vest, as though a lot of his time these days was dedicated to not damaging his career prospects in a country where the ruling majority don't often pretend to love the Chinese swelling minority.

In that prison interview room I was also being very careful about what I said for a microphone that could be in the bulbless lampholder suspended directly above the scrubbed table. The right words, or any words, are not easy to find when you have absolutely no idea whether or not the man you are interviewing is guilty of the charge which has landed him in prison. Ming had put the facts in front of me without making any claims about his client's innocence.

Li was keeping his eyes focused on the tabletop. He showed no interest in what I was saying and might not have been listening. There was just nothing about this man to suggest the boy who had once been so sure of himself and his own future, confident that he wasn't going to repeat even the relatively few mistakes his father had made. It had been the kind of extreme self-assurance which leaves you more or less naked to any wind of disaster.

On the flight to Malaysia there had been plenty of time for me to regret an impulse of years ago which was really the reason behind this return to the land of my birth. I had left Singapore for France after a total sell-up of everything, my cargo fleet long since gone, and my Johore factory, which made small boat engines, experiencing considerable problems from Korean competition, with the result that I got a poor price for it. I did a lot better with property in Singapore, this including my last home in the Far East, a local consortium having an eye on the site for a skyscraper, which they proceeded to build. I had arrived at my newly acquired villa in France determined to set about making a completely Western life for myself. Then, when I had been living with that scenario for personal happiness for about eighteen months, one of my oldest Chinese friends, Li Wong Tang, had suddenly turned up together with twenty-two year old Li Fong Chi, the son and heir he had fathered in his declining years, having had the misfortune previously to achieve only girls.

With old Wong I had been very near to a partnership a couple of times but we had both wisely decided that friendship was something you didn't throw away by going into business together. I had welcomed father and son to France without even a tremor of unease that they might be wanting anything more than a renewal of an agreeable relationship, but before lunch was over I learned that my friends had come to get money. This was quite a shock. I was glad then that I had broken the rule dictated by a slightly uncertain liver and had enjoyed two large gins as an apéritif; serious disillusion was always faced up to best when cushioned by alcohol.

They wanted my money to help them build an hotel. It had seemed to me, before I left the country, that this was the type of development that Malaysia needed least. Also, they planned to locate their project on a strip of the east coast facing the China Sea which, by some miracle, had until then been largely overlooked by developers.

The Trengannu seaboard is almost all beach, a long undulating stretch of white-gold sand behind which are rustling casuarinas and tall palms unbroken by hurricanes. The road to this paradise used to be a bad one, aggressively resistant to motor traffic. It wound through little *kampongs* where large grey, coconut-picker monkeys sat waiting for work at the end of long chains, all of them with wrinkled foreheads as though they spent their lives worrying about how to switch jobs with their owners. The owners were just bright enough to keep this from happening.

For years one of those private dreams you keep tucked away from public view had been that I would build my final home on this coast, a modest place, not more than eight to ten rooms up on stilts against the pythons waiting to join me, palm-thatched, but with air-conditioning, all this a carefully manufactured private paradise in which I would live out my days in a state of deep, internal stillness. Instead I got a windy terrace in France and a couple of Chinese visitors wanting money.

I ought to have said no firmly over the Brie and biscuits. Maybe I shouldn't have had three glasses of wine after the gin, or perhaps it was the sight of Chinese faces again which unstoppered sentimentality. I remember that I found myself wanting to talk about the place they were about to despoil, even inquiring tenderly after those monkeys,

discovering that they were still there, technology as yet not
having evolved a more efficient and cost-effective method
of harvesting coconuts. So I looked at their plans for the
hotel, staring at these while I was talked at steadily by the
elder Li, whose English couldn't keep up with his enthusiasm, forcing him to lapse into a kind of patois of Malay
studded with Chinese phrases. He had always tended to
talk like that, unable to stabilize into any one language.

The trouble with those plans was that they looked all
right and, allied to a chorus of conservationist talk from the
two Lis, I began to get a little trickle-breeze of a feeling
that maybe the old man was right, and that this was a
commercial proposition with moral overtones. That should
have made me suspicious. I've seen enough of what happens to moral overtones in business to know at what point
you say good day and make for the exit.

Li senior's theme music for me was that he was not really
proposing to build a hotel at all, what he had in mind was
a new kind of holiday community which in no way would
be commercializing that beautiful coast, instead offering
sanctuary for the needy rich. To this place would come the
heartsick and world-weary and, almost at once, as they
unpacked, they would find that their neuroses didn't come
out of the suitcases along with their Hawaiian shirts and
those large bandannas so useful for ladies not allowed to go
topless in a predominantly Muslim country.

It was inevitable that other holiday resorts were going to
appear on that coast, and it was really the responsible citizen's duty to set a pattern for later developments, one in
which the aesthetic figured hugely, a harmonious blending
of man's construction with surrounding nature. Didn't I
see, Li senior wondered in a shout, the trouble he had gone
to for these effects? The architect had been brought down
from Japan and stayed a month while his creative sensibili-
ties got in tune with the environmental situation. This put

in pidgin Chinese-Malay-English, and in a shrill voice, was somehow persuasive, as was also the suggestion that the alternative to the Li syndicate's restrained cultural project could well be hotels going up to ten storeys above the tallest palm trees, their frontages decorated with glued-on sun balconies.

All that my two guests wanted from me in this dedicated campaign to save an as yet unpolluted Tregannu coast for posterity was half a million US dollars. This would give me a share in the project and an income from the customer inflow. I had only to hand over the money; I wouldn't be expected to play anything like an active role, not be troubled at all, continuing to sit happily on my French terrace looking out at the Mediterranean, secure in the knowledge that my investment was bringing me in the kind of return I'd never get from the stock exchange.

I still don't know why I fell for it. Perhaps it was because of all those cut strings to Malaysia hanging over the edge of my new life, and I had secretly wanted again just one string to which I would never take the scissors. Old Li didn't get his half a million dollars, he got two hundred thousand. I had no income from the investment for three years after the hotel was built, and from then on this golden financial opportunity had always resulted in considerably less income than I would have received from a conservative British building society or US mutuals.

Old Li had talked about a sleeping directorship for me, but I was never actually offered this, not even for the distinction of my name on their notepaper. Then the old man died, and had a huge, traditional funeral which I did not attend, this with paper automobiles and all the trimmings, including weeping mourners paid by the hour. A couple of years later young Li had worked himself up to hotel manager, for which achievement I didn't bother to send my congratulations.

Now we were sitting in a jail interview room facing each other while I struggled to get answers that Li either wasn't able to give, or didn't want to. The back of his own hands seemed to fascinate him, almost as though by staring at them he could hold himself in a semi-hypnotic trance. It was a total surprise when suddenly he looked up, straight at me, then said in English:

'Mr Harris! They will hang me! Here in this place!'

CHAPTER 2

When the British Raj were pushed out of Malaysia the country became a kingdom, which was a bit of a surprise, as was also the compromise reached between local Sultans about who was to have the throne. It was agreed that this should be shared among the top families on a rota basis, with a fixed term of office, after which one king automatically retired with a new man taking over. So far this arrangement seems to have worked very well. It offers all the attractive pomp and ceremony stemming from a royal house without the very real problem of one reign lasting too long, something that gets boring even for the most faithful of subjects.

If there are any disadvantages to the king by rotation system it could be that in a small country there will soon be a really noticeable number of people about the place who can claim royal connections either from present or past reigns. My former business associate Batim Salong was one of these. I had never asked him, and I don't think he would have liked it if I had, just where he stood in line to one of the thrones, but he had always had a kind of regal aura about him, this particularly noticeable when he was travelling abroad.

In trouble we all of us look to our influential friends, and the morning after my arrival in KL my passport went missing. I found out about this after breakfast when I went up to my room to get that document you need to hire a self-drive car in foreign countries. After the previous day's Customs inspection on the train at the Singapore–Malaysia frontier I had put my passport back in the attaché case where it lives and locked the case. I had never unlocked it in my hotel bedroom, but someone else had, and with no marks at all on the lock flap, this suggesting a professional.

My passport is never in my wallet because I don't believe in all my travel eggs in one basket. Also, though I carry a couple of credit cards, I am not an enthusiast, preferring the currency of the country I am in on the principle that a thinning wad of notes is a steady reminder of how much you are spending, while credit cards were born out of the live-now-pay-next-year culture. I had worn my wallet down to breakfast as a weight in the inside pocket of a jacket carried over my arm, which meant that, though I had lost my identity while I ate, I still had the money that would buy it back again. Or so I thought.

The first thing to do was ring Batim. His number is unlisted, but I've had it for years, and even used it from France once or twice, much more easily than I was to use it from the capital of his country. I dialled and waited. There were the usual clicks from an automatic exchange followed by a kind of sighing noise, as though a computer somewhere was only just recovering from a deep personal grief. Silence, then more clicks, followed by a voice, male, asking what I wanted.

'*Apa hajat?*'

'Can you speak English?'

'Sure,' said the voice.

'I take it you are His Excellency Batim Salong's secretary?'

He didn't admit to that, serving me silence. So I let him have the spiel, really without any clue as to whether he was listening.

'You've got that?' I asked, at the end.

'Sure.'

'Well, will you now please put me on to your employer?'

'Not,' said the voice.

'Look! I am a former business partner of His Excellency. He has stayed as my guest in France. Just give him my name. It is Paul Harris. Got that?'

There was the thump of the phone being put down. The computer came in again, sighing, though more softly this time, not much more than a heavy breathing. Then the voice, sudden, abrupt:

'Not.'

'What do you mean—"not"?'

'Not speak.'

The line went dead. I re-dialled, got the clicks, the sighing, but no bell rang at the other end. After that I called the desk in the lobby and told them to get the police.

I got the manager first, who arrived in defence of his staff, all of whom he had known since they were babes in arms and all utterly incapable of stealing so much as a candy bar. I could have dropped my passport somewhere, it was an easy thing to do, especially since I did not carry it with my money. It was fortunate, wasn't it, that I had lost no money? Also, I had said that the case had been locked when I came back from breakfast. Did I think that any of his employees would have the skill to open my case without leaving any scratch marks on the lock? Looking at the specimens of his staff he had brought with him, two maids, one of them weeping, and the waiter who had delivered whisky the night before, I took his point. By this time the manager was using his hands, and I was beginning to feel like a throwback to an old-fashioned colonial imperialist of the type which the Far East had finally shaken off its back and hoped to forget entirely. The man ended by wondering what I thought one of his hotel staff could possibly want with *my* passport, of all things?

I got the answer to that when the police finally arrived, this the result of my stubborn insistence that they be called. It was well past 11.0 a.m. before the law finally knocked on my door. They had arrived without sirens, that kind of screeching up to an hotel entrance being bad for the tourist trade. I rated two policemen, one in crisp uniform, the other wearing a not too smart tropic two-piece which, if it had been put on fresh that morning, was already wilting. I was dealt with by the man in the suit, while the uniformed visitor had a look around, apparently particularly interested in the bathroom.

As a kind of by-product of my career I have had quite a lot to do with the police in assorted countries and these days I can't quite get away from the feeling that forces throughout the world are tending to develop a new type of officer who no longer believes that any crime can be solved if you really work at it. A different concept of law and order appears to have taken over; that an approved success ratio is the thing to aim for, more or less a fixed percentage of criminals captured. And, provided that this percentage doesn't drop too heavily in any one year, there really isn't too much to worry about.

The detective-sergeant might have had a rough yesterday, with only eight hours' sleep between it and me, but he still achieved a very civil patience. When he had heard the hotel manager out on that theme of the utter trustworthiness of the hotel staff he sent the man away and cleared the room, including the uniformed policeman. I was then told, more or less in confidence, that it was perfectly possible, indeed even likely, that my room had been burgled while I was eating breakfast. This kind of thing did happen now and then, with visitors' passports, rather than their money, often the target. It was all part of the drug trade which Malaysia is fighting so determinedly with the death sentence. Westerners' passports, just slightly doctored for the use of couriers in the cocaine trade, had a high market value. However, I was not to be greatly troubled, I had my money and I would find that the British High Commission in Kuala Lumpur would be able to fix me up with something temporary.

He gave me a warm smile and a parting thought.

'So, Mr Harris, no great trouble for you.'

I wasn't too sure about that. A feeling of instability hangs around my national status, which could mean the High Commission, or the Consulate, not doing anything like a rush job on my particular case. I was brought up as a British subject living in the Far East whose father had been born in Scotland, this more or less by accident because my grandmother had happened to be there when it happened. I was born in the old Malaya under the Union Jack, national identity clear enough, but I had rather mucked this up many years later by becoming a citizen of the new Republic of Singapore, mainly because it was going to be good for business. Lee Kwan Yew, the Prime Minister, wouldn't accept me as one of his own unless I renounced allegiance to Queen Elizabeth II, which I proceeded to do. Then, when I decided to live in France, it seemed a good idea to become British again, since there was just no way I could pretend to be French. To say that Britain welcomed me back with open arms would be an overstatement. At first I got a very dusty answer, no doubt deserved, but finally, by a devious route nearly as complicated as getting a divorce from the Vatican—and almost as expensive—I am once again nominally under the shelter of the Queen, I suspect without being rated as one of her most deeply loved subjects.

As I had suspected, High Commissions have no more power than Embassies to help the traveller in trouble and appear to have even less desire to do so. It wasn't a great deal better at the Consulate where the man behind the desk at first looked slightly relieved that I hadn't come asking for money. He was about to go off for his lunch at the Selangor Club and told me so. They are trained to say no with a smile, but this sub-vice-consul couldn't manage the smile on account of being in desperate need of the day's first Tiger beer. Even patience was decidedly frayed at the edges.

'Look, Mr Harris, there is just no way I can issue any document that will let you hire a self-drive car. To put it frankly, we don't know who the hell you are until we have had a thorough check-up and your home domicile in France isn't going to help with that little problem. As for those credit cards, they don't begin to establish anyone's identity, certainly not in the Far East.'

'Is there anything you *can* do for me?'

He thought about that.

'Well, we could probably get you out of the country all right. As an undesirable alien. Particularly since you can pay for your air seat. I can get to work on that for you if you like. After lunch. Come back here about three.'

'Thanks. I don't want to be deported.'

He stood up.

'Then I'm sorry. I've got to go now. Just fill in these three forms and leave them with my secretary. That'll start the machine clanking.'

'Slowly?' I suggested.

He smiled for the first time.

'That's right. It's what keeps chaps like me in full employment. Oh, I forgot. One thing more. In view of what's happened it might be a good idea to go back to the police for a chitty you can use in lieu of passport. Some hotels demand passports on registration, then put the things in their safes. Can be quite trying. Especially if you have a dirty weekend in mind.'

'A police chitty wouldn't get me a self-drive?'

'I doubt it. Why do you want to drive yourself anyway?'

'I have a thing about being driven.'

'Much safer out here. Knock someone over and the legal proceedings can be a lifetime project. Particularly if your victim is a Malay. 'Bye.'

I had a curry lunch before I went back to the police for the chitty, which was just as well, because the sunset was imminent by the time I got back to my hotel. I was tired and lay down on the bed to think, but went to sleep instead. The phone bell woke me. I fumbled around for the handset.

'Yes? Paul Harris.'

There was a throat clearing noise, then a voice I knew.

'I'm sending a car for you. Ten tomorrow morning.'

'That's charming of you, Batim. Do you never answer your unlisted number yourself these days?'

He hung up.

CHAPTER 3

When I first met Batim he was beautiful. He had the kind of dark loveliness which stunned women as he walked across an hotel foyer, with here and there a man catching his breath as well. In those days Batim rarely travelled with less than two cars, both Bentleys. He had come to consider a Rolls vulgar, and left these to Chinese towkays. His entourage tended to consist of at least eight retainers, sometimes including his latest girlfriend likely to be wearing an outsize ruby on one side of her nose.

However, as a beauty he had known an even shorter run

than most. By twenty-six a weight blurring had started up around his jowls and by thirty it wasn't his half-inch black eyelashes you noticed so much, more the red veining on his eyeballs. I was received by a host slumped on a lounger in a manner which did nothing to flatter what had once been an Adonis body. He had apparently been in the pool for he was wearing outsize swimming trunks, a towel over his shoulders and a pair of dark glasses. Nature had left him with most of the hair on his head, and he was apparently still vain about this; it had been carefully cut, if on the long side. Though his head was lifted, because of those glasses, I couldn't see whether he was looking at me or just the house façade.

'I knew you'd come back, you bastard,' he said.

Though there were plenty of seats around I went on standing, gaining perhaps a small advantage from this. I had travelled to Batim's jungle retreat in an ancient Ford I suspected was only used when it was necessary to bring third-class visitors here for an audience. It wouldn't have surprised me to learn that my driver had been ordered to use minor roads all the way to make quite certain that no one who mattered would see who was in the back seat.

'Sit down,' Batim said.

When I had he took off his glasses the better to assess change in an old colleague and semi-friend. He put them on again in seconds, and with eyes hidden was once again slightly sinister, almost suggesting a Mafia boss still keeping sharply in touch with business interests from a Florida hideaway defended by hungry alligators.

He said: 'Seeing you in France that time had me laughing in my air seat all the way back here.'

The reference was to a meeting four years earlier on my flower-decked terrace behind the glitter coast.

'Remember what you told me about how you were spending your time in France?' he asked.

'No.'

'You said you were playing an exciting game of losing money on the Tokyo, Hong Kong, and London stock markets. But you hadn't got around to playing the New York market. Have you got around to it?'

'I've run out of playmoney.'

'So what else do you do? Get up early to go down to the pâtisserie for your croissants?'

'I study Chinese,' I said.

'What the hell for? You were going to become a European.'

'I've always felt illiterate in Mandarin. Even in France that went on troubling me. There were only a couple of hundred idiographs I could put any kind of meaning to. So now I've got a target of a thousand.'

'Your mind will go before you reach it,' Batim said. 'Damn waste of good living time.'

When we were in business together I had found it useful to know how to push my colleague at least part of the way towards one of his decidedly distinguished rages. Almost anything Chinese could be used for that purpose. As I had thought it might, this still worked. He was starting to get restive on the lounger. He muttered: 'Mandarin!'

'The coming language out here,' I said. 'And before long all around the Pacific basin. It's something that's going to revolutionize the communications industry. There is just no way you can program a computer memory into dealing with seventeen different spoken inflections that put totally new meanings to a single ideograph. You can't do it with Fax either. So for the business man it is going to be back to the abacus and long-distance phone calls in Mandarin. In time it will happen in Europe as well.'

'Paul! Shut up!'

For a good two minutes after that my host said nothing, which gave me time to look around. This rural retreat that

Batim used to call a cottage when he was travelling abroad as an official representative of the Asian toiling masses, hadn't changed all that much. There was some new pool-side furniture and, stretching to the outer defensive wall, a row of what appeared to be white marble urns holding canna lilies that were a lot better than my French ones, these pointing straight up towards a cloudless sky.

The rich in tropic climes are still mostly unaffected by a social conscience, they don't try to hide the numbers of servants ministering to the boss's every whim. Beyond the urns were the bent backs of gardeners working on the weeds that kept seeding in from the jungle. At the doors to the main reception room, alongside ten-foot-high sliding glass panels, was a man in a white turban who just stood there, waiting for orders. On my last visit some of the household staff had been in combat green with automatic rifles practically at the ready, this the consequence of a flare-up of Red guerrilla trouble, but apparently the country had once again been made safe for the upper classes. I hadn't seen a gun anywhere, not even racked in the front hall.

From the way Batim's head moved I guessed he was looking at me again. He made a pronouncement:

'You hate living in France.'

It wasn't all that shrewd an assessment, the facts had been fairly obvious at the time of his Riviera visit. Even back then I was becoming geographically restive and slightly testy, insisting on eating inside with all the windows shut against the howling breeze, and quite often with the blinds dropped on the view. My fellow émigrés from various parts of the world, but mostly rich Germans and Scandinavians, were beginning to suggest that what I needed was a yacht, preferably quite a big one, to have something serious to worry about.

I didn't want a yacht, certainly not in the Mediterranean. When I did go out on my terrace I kept staring at that sea

with the world's highest effluent content, realizing that as
a piece of water it had nothing to say to me. But I have a
stubborn streak from Scots ancestors which demands that
I stick to a decision made, this almost to the point of pain.
Changing your mind about something to which you have
solemnly committed yourself is practically as bad as deny-
ing the Presbyterian doctrine of the Predestination of All
Souls.

Batim raised a hand and the man in white came over
from the doorway to present his master with a cigarette,
then to light it for him, after which the servant retired again
to his waiting and watching. Even though I wasn't directly
facing the man I was conscious of being under observation.
You need training from youth up to be able to ignore the
staring of many servants, and I had never had this, my
father being Scots about wasting money on people you
didn't really need in the house. I remember my mother
once suggesting that she could use a personal maid, to
which my pa's reaction had been a very loud: 'Nonsense!'

Batim really savoured his tobacco, having long since
signed a pledge against booze and the sins of youth. His
lungs took a long time to get rid of the fumes and after a
slow exhalation he practically sighed a question which anyone but me might have taken as a special politeness.

'Come by Singapore, did you?'

'It was the only way I could. All the KL flights were
booked.'

'And you were in a great hurry?' he suggested. 'What do
you think of your city these days?'

'I don't care for all those skyscrapers. They'll soon have
to build a museum Chinatown.'

He had another session with his cigarette, then came in
to the attack, but with his voice still deceptively gentle.

'What made you decide to come bleating to me about
your lost passport?'

I smiled at him.

'Been making a few inquiries to the police, have you?'

'Naturally. I used to do it quite often in my dealings with you. But you haven't answered my question.'

'I rang you, Batim, because no one in KL will rent a car to a foreigner who has lost his documentation.'

He did the smiling then.

'Imagine Paul Harris not knowing where to go in KL backstreets to get what he wants.'

'There aren't any backstreets left up here either. Just more of those damn skyscrapers. Batim, a word from you down the phone would have got me a hire car.'

He didn't deny this, just offered a smile. His teeth were still beautiful.

'You could have rung down to your hotel desk for a car with a chauffeur,' he suggested. 'But you've never much cared for the idea of a witness to what you were up to.'

I smiled back at him. The friendship side of our long relationship seemed to be coming up strong. He offered me a non-alcoholic drink.

'I'd prefer a gin,' I said.

'None of that stuff in this house.'

'It wasn't always so,' I told him.

He ignored that, shouting to the man in white. Very soon I was brought a concoction which seemed to be made from squashed guavas, or perhaps rambutans. The taste was horrible. Batim watched me sip. He might have been a medico in a home for inebriates, interested in a patient's reaction to a new miracle cure. He then decided that I was entitled to an explanation of why he hadn't immediately come to my aid. He was sure I would understand that he simply couldn't have it put about in Kuala Lumpur that he was in contact with a man whose business partner was in jail on a charge of dealing in cocaine.

'Li is not and never has been my partner.'

'How would you prefer to be classified? Sleeping partner?'

The time had come to state plainly why I had come back to Malaysia, whether or not Batim was prepared to believe me. He listened politely until it was time for his comment.

'So it was a woman's cry of distress which brought you back to us, Paul? I can remember that when you were living out here there was talk that your motivation could be quite humanitarian at times. I'm bound to say that in our long contact I never saw a shred of evidence to support this. However, I'll pretend to believe you.' He paused before adding: 'I think your man Li is going to hang.'

'I'm prepared to bring an English Queen's Counsel out here to defend him.'

'I doubt if you'd be allowed to do that. And if it was permitted that would be making Li's execution a certainty.'

He got up from the lounger, not without a certain difficulty, as though being overweight had somehow upset his sense of balance.

'It's time for lunch,' he said. 'I'll send you to Kuantan, Paul. After dinner tonight.'

'Darkness defending your reputation?'

'Correct.'

At table Batim demonstrated that whatever joys of this world he had decided to give up to improve his chances in the next, food wasn't one of them. His purpose over a Java curry was serious, my host periodically raising a finger to have a volcano cone of rice on his plate maintained at its original height, this frequently topped off with a fresh lava-flow of vegetables, chicken meat and seafood. Long after I had reached the fruit Batim carried on with his devotions. Then, quite suddenly, I was given a lizard stare from half-hooded eyes.

'Paul, I thought you'd sold up everything before you went to France?'

'I did.'

'What about that boat you used to keep at Kuantan?'

'I sold that, too. A fisherman bought it.'

'I see. Well, a fisherman doesn't have it now. It belongs to your hotel. I seem to remember it had remarkable engines. Capable of high speeds. Not the sort of boat you need for tourists, really. Didn't Li let you know he had bought it?'

'Li and I hadn't been in contact for years.'

Batim switched attention back to his plate.

CHAPTER 4

Perhaps as a reward for having listened to him all afternoon on the subject of the forces undermining contemporary Malaysian society, i.e. the Chinese, Batim despatched me to Kuantan not in the old Ford, but in a Bentley. It was well after 11.0 p.m. when I left, by then long dark, and a moonless night as well. I had protested that all I needed was transport back to the city and my hotel, but my host insisted that I must travel to the other side of the country in total comfort. When I pointed out that this would probably mean arriving in Kuantan somewhere around 5.0 a.m. he said that this was an ideal time to come swooping down on my Trengannu investment to test out whether or not my staff were being kept on their toes by whoever was currently running the place.

The limo was certainly comfortable. I settled into the back seat and waved through tinted glass to Batim at the front door supervising my departure. We moved away without the faintest sound of a gear change and no hum at all from the air-conditioning. I decided that a Bentley is a

delightful compromise when you wish to avoid the ostenta-
tion of a Rolls, exactly the same job except for the radiator
and, of course, minus the vulgarity of that statuette of a
lady with wings. I had another thought, too, this being that
in spite of an alcohol-less evening I would soon be asleep.

The glass screen between the front and back seats was
lowered, but there had to be a button somewhere that
would raise it. I considered looking for this to punch it and
protect the driver from my snores, then realized that this
could be interpreted as a symbolic throwback to the days
of the wicked Raj. It took me some moments to be quite
sure that the man up front was the man who had brought
me from KL. In the Ford he had been on the scruffy side,
capless and giving off more than a slight suggestion of being
underwashed, but now he was as impeccably uniformed as
a captain on his bridge. There was also a huge difference
in his driving technique. In the Ford I had several times
been near to commenting on how his testing out of aged
shock absorbers made it rough going in the back, but I
wasn't paying for the transport so had kept quiet. Now his
performance was impeccable, and we slid through the
tropic night behind floodlights beamed ahead, towering
jungle on both sides hanging over us like huge, black waves
about to break.

I was just nodding off when there was a voice from up
front. The man who had brought me from KL offering
no more than half-surly grunts in reply to my occasional
politeness was now apparently determined to be sociable.
It might be something expected of him when he was in the
smart uniform. And he was attempting English.

'How you live Malaysia?'

I am not a patient man. If there was once even a fragment
of the teacher instinct in my genes I suppressed it early.
This fellow knew perfectly well, since he must have heard
me using it at my hotel, that I spoke reasonable if slightly

rusty Malay, and if his object was to strike up a new friendship in the middle of a dark night when his attention should
have fixed on steering this vehicle, then he ought to have
set about it more modestly, in Malay. It was not my intention to spend the long hours en route to the east coast in a
kind of mobile tutorial.

I said, in Malay: 'I was born here.'

I waited, but not for long. He was stubborn.

'So? You make good lifes?'

'Only one,' I said in English, teaching in spite of myself.

I thought that had switched him off. We went through a
kampong where some lights were still burning. In spite of
the insulated windows I heard a dog bark. Five minutes
later the chauffeur started up in Malay, and I listened to a
monologue going on for minutes without a pause to let me
insert a word. Not that I wanted to.

Even with a Bentley to drive the man up front couldn't
begin to feel that he had the ideal life. In the first place it
wasn't his Bentley and, in the second, his wife had left him.
He asked if I had a wife but allowed me no gap in which
to answer, going on about what it was like to have your
woman suddenly one day just roll up her possessions into
a huge bundle and put this, plus their child, into a taxi in
which she had been driven back to her native village, leaving him to pay the bill for her journey.

Sleep was off the agenda. I came under a verbal barrage
from which I could only escape by pushing a button to lift
the partition, but I didn't do that, humane even under
fatigue stress. Those outpourings from a damaged ego had
no effect on his driving which remained beyond criticism,
speedometer needle hovering at sixty-five, engine noise
scarcely a kitten-purr. It was almost as though the Bentley,
in its flawless mechanical operation, was the only true per-
fection he had encountered in twenty-seven years of living.

He told me he was a prisoner in Malaysia, serving a life

sentence. He had no hope of ever getting away unless by some miracle he had highly influential help from outside the country. When he thought of the whole world out there waiting beyond the boundaries of this little country, and countless things he would never see, it just burned him up. On top of this restlessness of spirit was another huge problem, which he would tell me about since I was so understanding. His name was Mahmud, and I was bound from that to think that he was pure Malay, but he wasn't, he was half Chinese.

That was a surprise. I could scarcely believe that Batim, knowingly, would ever employ anyone with even a fraction of Chinese blood let alone fifty per cent of the stuff. And then it hit me that this was just the kind of thing my old colleague might do, setting racial prejudice to one side where his personal interests were concerned. It wasn't at all a bad way to buy loyalty from a servant in a country where, increasingly, those who aren't guaranteed Malays run the risk of being labelled second-class citizens.

Mahmud said he was deeply grateful to the man who had given him a new life and had him trained as a Rolls-Bentley maintenance mechanic down in Singapore, but in spite of this good fortune he remained basically insecure. As he put it simply, Batim was a man whose heart might explode at any time and if that happened where would his chauffeur be? These days the market in Malaysia for highly trained chauffeurs was getting very thin, even the rich going for owner-driving.

After the confessional Mahmud did the decent thing, offering me the return therapy of his listening ear. He started rather subtly, saying he had once read a book about France, this written in English which he had learned at school. The book had interested him greatly. I was expecting an inquiry about the likely numbers of rich men in France who might be willing to employ Mahmud after

Batim's heart had exploded, but that didn't turn out to be
his line. He wanted to know why I had chosen to live there.
I thought of saying for the food, but settled for the climate.
There were no impertinent questions about the women in
my life, though he did seem very interested in my domestic
arrangements, which could have been leading up to
whether or not I had a Bentley in the garage. I said I drove
a small Fiat. If that was a disappointment he rallied from
it well, making the suggestion that I travelled a great deal.
Was I often in Paris? From what he sensed about me he
was sure that I was a very social man who would have
many visitors to stay and many houses in which I was
always a welcome guest. His intuitive understanding of my
patterns and character was a long way off beam, but if he
wanted to have me a Riviera playboy I could see no harm
in it. I began to feed him tasty little scraps from my French
experience. He pounced on these like a hungry terrier,
wanting more.

If I hadn't been so tired, as well as feeling heavy from
that Java curry, I might have sensed much sooner that
Mahmud had been briefed for this contact with me, though
perhaps inadequately. Not to cause him any alarm, or even
give him the feeling that he was failing in his assignment,
I didn't cut him off, just allowed the talk between us to
dribble away into silence. And if he found this upsetting he
didn't let it show. Perhaps he was also exhausted.

It was pushing 2.0 a.m. when we started to glide down
city steets, the suburban ones empty. Even near the centre
of the capital it was too late for the night-time parade of
young men walking side by side followed by giggling girls.
There were no other cars on the sweep up to my hotel
portico, and only a few in the parking area. I let myself out
of the Bentley, Mahmud making no move to open the door
for me. From the hotel steps I said:

'I left my bags at reception. I've only got to pay for my

room. Shouldn't take ten minutes. You don't need to park
the car.'

I went up and through revolving doors into a lobby gone
dead prior to the arrival of cleaners. There was a reception
light on but no one behind the desk. Mahmud had shown
no sign of coming into the hotel to help me with my
bags and perhaps it was a slight irritation from this which
made me look back through the glass doors. The Bentley
was no longer under the brightly lit portico. I went out
on to the steps again, watching the car being tucked into
a corner of the parking area. Its lights went out. I could
just see the shape of Mahmud getting out of the front
and into the back.

A light came on in the car. I went down steps to the
parking area, in shadow until I reached the almost total
shelter of a Citroën station-wagon. Even through the
Bentley's tinted glass I could see that Mahmud was using
a car phone. He seemed to be doing the talking, once or
twice gesticulating with a free hand.

I went back into the hotel. The night clerk had woken
up and was manning reception. He had my bags ready and
my bill, slightly confused by my sudden change of plan.
However, Kuala Lumpur suffers from an excess of rooms
over the demand for them, so the man was most agreeable
about booking me in for another night. I had to do my own
transporting of a large suitcase plus a smaller one up to the
fourth floor where my new accommodation had a slightly
different décor from the bedroom I'd had before. In the bathroom the light over the washbasin mirror wasn't working,
but I didn't mention this when I rang down to reception to
say that if a man in a chauffeur's uniform came in asking for
me he was to put him through on the phone.

I had my jacket and shoes off and my pyjamas unpacked
when the buzzing came. It was Mahmud in something of
a state, using English again.

'Why you do such things?'

I explained that for the last half-hour or so in the car I had felt a headache threatening and the thought of carrying my luggage down to the car park had made me quite dizzy, so I realized that I simply couldn't face the long night drive to Kuantan. In the morning I would get a hire car and driver to take me the rest of the way. I would ring his employer with a complete explanation, so he wasn't to let what was happening trouble him in any way.

Mahmud's reaction to this gentle kindness was a complete silence. I could hear him breathing. I thanked him for having driven me with such care this far on my journey. I said good-night and put down the phone.

CHAPTER 5

My hire car the next morning was one of those early Japanese jobs built when they still hadn't quite got the message and were trying to take over world markets with models given flower names like Daisy and Petunia. My journey was not comfortable, and the only thing to be said for my driver was that if he had acute personal problems he kept quiet about them. He spoke very little, giving the impression that he was totally fascinated by his own driving skills, having evolved little games to play on long trips, like how close he could come to the restraining stone walls on cliffside S-bends without actually testing the car's front fenders for rust content.

We made good time, a trip from which I emerged with aching bones and a thinned-down wad of banknotes. It was a moment or two before I really noticed where I was, which turned out to be in a clump of palm trees suitably equipped with coconuts high up, but no sign of monkeys waiting to go on duty. In spite of my general condition the part hotel-owner in me made an immediate note of this failure to exploit a visitor amenity. In the Highlands of Scotland they now have large dogs carefully trained to come out from the front doors of baronial mansion hotels offering friendly tailwags of welcome. If you don't like dogs you don't come back; but on the whole this innovation has gone down splendidly as a selling factor, guests tending to remember the lovely canines and to forget about the plumbing. Where there are coconut palms there ought to be monkeys, otherwise how are people suffering from actute travel fatigue going to be able to appreciate that they are actually on holiday in the real tropics?

Being left alone with my large case and smaller one then put me smack up against my second criticism of the Pindong Hotel arrival area. There was no one to carry my luggage. I had not arrived at 5.0 a.m. as Batim had intended but in the early afternoon, when life at a holiday hotel, if not exactly swinging, should still be in a reasonably active phase. The welcome facilities were clearly inadequate. At this point for new arrivals a progressive management ought to offer the happy shock of a smiling youth, wearing a cap advertising the place, coming running to help with bags and advice. For a minute or so I stood hoping to be surprised, then picked up my cases.

The path lay over an imitation Japanese footbridge across a creek which seemed to be travelling at ooze pace from the nearby jungle. I took another pause to have a proprietorial look around. The architect from Kyoto had done such a good job making the whole place blend in with nature that it was difficult to identify the admin block. Beyond the bridge other little paths ran in almost every direction, all equipped with signs bearing painted arrows, most apparently leading back under palms and past screens of casuarina trees to what could very well be your extremely private tent deep in the rain forest. Then I located one central exception, a construction that went up for two floors. As though in shame that he had been obliged to do this, the creative artist from Japan must have insisted that the necessary edifice be hidden by a row of banana palms. Over a few years these had grown to the point where they were no longer economic as fruit producers, having concentrated on leaves, all out for the world shelter-belt record. Only two pieces of roof were still visible.

Standing on that footbridge, I was beginning to understand why for years I had received no returns on my investment, even now only getting the kind of percentage on capital which tends to suggest that a liquidator could be lurking in the wings. Much as I hate sun balconies, I wasn't sure that I cared for the casuarina and banana palm alternative. The big emphasis seemed to be on shade, far too much of it, a distant shine of sand on a beach just visible, but up here in the complex there was more than a suggestion of prime mosquito-breeding territory, everything the malaria-carrying insect requires, including sluggish water. In our litiginous age the idea of hotel guests exposed to this threat was really frightening.

I put down my bags inside what had to be the lobby, finding myself in Tarzan country, that is if Tarzan ever came down out of trees to use a cave. The builders must have opened a special quarry to get all the rocks for the place, some of them almost pyramid block size, but left rough. Subsidiary caves housed reception and offered passages off, one of these with a sign saying 'Kelantan Bar'. The whole area needed daytime lighting, but none was switched on. There was, however, a loud, steady hum from an air-conditioning plant squandering electricity to produce the kind of chill which came near to freezing the sweat that had travelled with me from Kuala Lumpur. Behind the reception sub-cave was a bead curtain screening what seemed to be a passage. A faint glow came through the beads that could be sunshine from a window.

I asked if there was anyone about to no reaction, so I ended up shouting. This finally produced a distant clicking of sandals. The clicking came to the bead curtain and stopped. I was being assessed by someone in the passage who might be thinking about pressing the hotel's general alarm button. A light came on in reception. The beads parted.

For me now anyone under thirty-five is a girl. This girl would have been quite pretty if she had been able to take the time to repair heat-damaged make-up. The state of her hair suggested recent sleep. She was a redhead with the kind of skin that should never be brought to the tropics, pinkish, sun-hating. The way she was continuing to assess me from beyond the beads had me feeling that I wasn't making a favourable first impression. Carrying suitcases had disheveled me, too. She spoke first.

'Can I help?'

Not a hint of that usual 'sir' for paying customers.

I said: 'I hope so. I want a room.'

'Have you a reservation?'

Still no 'sir'. I was beginning to get a feeling that was almost rejection. I was also thinking about all the money I had sunk in this place. I told her that I hadn't bothered to ring up from KL because so far in the country I hadn't found reservations were necessary.

She didn't seem to care for the suggestion that the Pindong Hotel wasn't so popular that they didn't have to sleep three to a bed. I was beginning to get just a little irritated myself.

'You don't keep reception permanently manned?' I suggested.

Her answer was sharpish.

'People never check in at this time. No one travels about during the big heat.'

'I used to,' I said. 'When I was earning my living in this country.'

Past history didn't interest her. She explained that the reason for the morgue quiet in the admin block was because everyone was either having a siesta in their quarters or resting in the shade down at the beach. Buffet lunch was always served there unless it was raining. Breakfast was a tray meal, which meant that the dining-room didn't usually open until seven in the evening. All this information about hotel routine suggested that I was going to be allowed to stay, though it was delivered without a hint that she had ever heard of the rule that in the hotel business your face should ache all the time from a good-for-trade smile.

The lady had moved to the counter. She lifted the padded black cover of what looked like one of those ledgers used for company accounts in pre-computer days. This was swung around for me to sign myself in. A page was mostly unsullied by customers' names except at the very bottom where a clear round hand stated that a Mr and Mrs Chi Wok Tee from Taiwan had arrived four days earlier and were apparently still here, for the departure date column was blank. So was the wide one inviting comments from guests. The Chinese are quick to become bitter about bad food, so nothing said so far about the cuisine could be a good sign, though they might be saving up venom for a departure blast.

I was given a pen and signed, filling in arrival date and address in France. I swung the book back to the lady. Her routine check on my registration suddenly became something rather different. A reading of my name and address didn't exactly cause blind panic, but there was unquestionably a shock factor. She didn't look at me as she picked up the pen I had laid down and fitted this carefully into its holder. She then closed the ledger before raising her head. Her voice came pitched a lot lower than it had been.

'Why didn't you let us know you were coming, Mr Harris?'

I told her about the loss of my passport and claimed that this had prevented me from making any firm plans. Then I asked what her role was in the hotel. There was a certain reluctance in the way she answered that.

'I used to be Mr Li's assistant. Now I'm acting manager.'

'You mean since his arrest?'

She nodded, looking at the lid of the ledger.

'Who appointed you? Mrs Li?'

'Oh no. I mean, we never see her. She never comes here. She never has.'

'So you just took over?'

She still didn't look up.

'Well, in a sort of way I suppose so.'

'Lucky you were here to do it.'

She looked at me then.

'I don't think luck comes into it, Mr Harris. Why didn't you call us from France to say that you were coming?'

'That would have meant everything carefully laid out to receive me.'

'I see,' she said.

I was sure she did. She suggested that after driving in the heat I would like to go to my room. She found a key and came out of reception, telling me as she did so that they always kept one unreserved room with the air-conditioning on just in case someone arrived who hadn't booked.

'That happens quite often?' I wondered.

'Well, now and then. This way, Mr Harris.'

We went through another bead curtain into a passage lined with painted hardboard instead of rocks, and out through a glazed door on to one of the paths fanning out towards chalets modestly covering their raw concrete with quick growing vines. As we walked along I tried a social note.

'At least there are no elevator problems in this hotel,' I said, choosing the American word for the Pacific Basin area. She chose the British.

'Don't you like lifts, Mr Harris?'

'I have this feeling I'm going to die in one. Stuck between the thirty-eighth and thirty-ninth floors. It's a form of claustrophobia.'

I asked her name. It was Josie McCollom.

'Scots connections, Miss McCollom?'

'Yes. But it has been quite some time.'

We reached what were to be my quarters. As well as the vines the camouflage over this one included a bank of giant ferns that looked like an ideal cobra-nesting site. By the door was a metal plaque saying 'Orchid Suite'. I asked Miss McCollom how long she had been working at the Pindong Hotel and she said three years. I didn't ask whether she liked the job.

The Orchid Suite looked what it probably was for much of the time, a perfect setting for extra-marital sex. There wasn't actually a mirror on the ceiling, or a waterbed with an electrically-operated mattress roller, just a very successful bid on the part of the decorator to give you the feeling, as you walked in with your chosen partner, that this was going to be where your really big Asia travel memories would be coming from. The basic theme was pink, this carried on right through to the orchids and the bottle of champagne certain to go pop on opening just to prove that it came from France and not Bangkok. I stood for a moment almost in reverence at the thought of old Li loving every minute of the development of this project. It seemed a great pity he hadn't lived longer to enjoy it instead of being taken

prematurely at the age of eighty-seven. About young Li I
didn't want to think at all.

I went into the bathroom. That was heavily under the
Kyoto influence, with a Japanese bath that had steps down
into it. You could sit in water looking at an alcove for formal
ornament which held a green vase that should have had a
branch of plum blossom sprouting from it, but didn't. Just
in case you had never in your life really washed yourself
Oriental clean there was a notice giving instructions on how
to set about this via the *ofuro* technique. A framed wall
chart told me that *ofuro* meant honourable bath, and then
proceeded firmly with instructions that on no account was
I to use soap down in there, but must do all basic washing
on the cement surround, only getting into the water to relax.
As far as I could see there was no jacuzzi attachment, which
meant that this area wasn't really suitable for late night
parties, though there was plenty of spare space in which to
hold one. To get the *ofuro* heated up you needed a twenty-
minute switch-on, but for those who didn't much care about
getting really clean there was also a shower behind another
bead curtain.

Miss McCollom hadn't come with me on my tour of
inspection and didn't seem too curious about how I was
reacting to all this splendour, but when I came out of the
bathroom she asked if there was anything I wanted from
room service, so I said sandwiches and coffee and she left
at once as though it was her pleasure to do so.

The Orchid Suite had its own conservatory, this beyond
a bedroom wall given over to sliding glass panels, though
only one of these actually slid. When I had found out how
to work the security lock I stepped out into a tropic sun
porch where the room attendant should have seen to an
open ventilator, but had not. I was whacked by the kind of
heat which makes you gasp and which I found out on a
thermometer was registering a humid ninety-nine. Ther-

mometers should not be hung in any part of a tropic hotel suite just in case the air-conditioning breaks down and suffering guests start wondering why they ever left home. Out on that porch were plants gone limp and more orchids wanting to die.

I got the ventilators open and also a door to the outside world, stepping through it into breathable air. There wasn't much of a view on account of overhanging casuarinas. Behind me, in the private hothouse, was a wicker sofa plus a featured fan-backed chair just in case I felt like pretending to be a Somerset Maugham character sitting in his lonely outpost with only a whisky soda for company plus a three-months-old copy of the *Daily Telegraph* which had just arrived by jungle runner.

I went back in for a shower, leaving the *ofuro* game for later, and must have been in the bathroom for fifteen minutes or so getting really cool, coming out wearing a pink towel as a sarong. I glanced towards the sunroom plants to see if they were beginning to recover from their ordeal and one broad-leafed variety appeared to be. Above it was a face.

If that face had just disappeared I might have thought it an hallucination from riding around in a hot automobile. But it stayed. It was female and Chinese, the body under it screened by reviving foliage. The lady was not young. She had black hair, probably dyed, pulled straight back to a bun I couldn't see. Sticking out from this was a jade ornament that might have been a hatpin. She could have been an amah from my youth in Singapore, that almost standard face which seems immune to all emotion and is only slightly marked by wrinkles.

The lady didn't move until I moved. By the time I had got into the sunroom and through the door I had left open, there was no trace of her. There were three sanded paths she could have used, each soon screened by the drooping feather branches of casuarinas.

I didn't think the old woman had been inside the bed-room but I still checked an open case for any hint of searching fingers. Nothing had been disturbed. I didn't feel that she had come to steal and somehow that long stare at me through glass had seemed more than just curiosity.

There was a knock on the main door of the Orchid Suite. Sandwiches and a pot of coffee were being delivered by a bright-eyed young man probably hurriedly retrieved from beach duty. He gave me the commercially trained smile of welcome.

'Good day. I Chong Fi, room boy. Welcome Pindong.'

CHAPTER 6

After a day of bouncing travel I should have had a sound night's sleep, but I didn't. A contributory factor to insomnia might have been my solitary occupancy of a whoreshop set. I'd had dinner alone out in the sunroom, bitten by mosquitoes that had come in while the transoms were open, seated in a fan-backed chair and eating by the light of a fat candle inside a glass globe.

I chose from a menu card while happy boy Chong stood alongside making suggestions accompanied by laughter that was possibly cynical comment on what I was being offered. My steak must have come from a water buffalo that had died of old age as it stood passive in a paddy field, and the salad reminded me of a long-ago Kuantan resthouse culinary tradition. Back in those days guests got, every night, the same raw offering of sliced onions and cucumbers dressed with vinegar and laid out on lettuce limp with heat exhaustion.

It wasn't indigestion that woke me, just the air-conditioning. I had lived with cooling systems in both my

Kuala Lumpur and Singapore houses, but at night there had always been a switch-off in the bedrooms. If you didn't do this you missed out completely on the physical experience which had made it possible for Europeans to survive and flourish right on the equator. Every morning about three the temperature drops so dramatically that, after sweating under a sheet, or no sheet, you reach down for a blanket. And if there is a 'Sumatra' squall with rain, maybe two blankets. It can be quite a joyous waking from hot sleep, especially if you aren't alone in the bed.

In the cities, with drainage control, mosquitoes are not a big problem, but here, if I opened a ventilator they were going to be. I went on lying under a pink, tropic-weight duvet, not able to escape from thought attack, this based on not much liking the hotel in which I had sunk more money than I could afford, plus a feeling that I was at least partially responsible for a development which looked like being considerably worse than most tourist flypaper projects. I lay in a too-cool bed hoping that the paper money and the paper houses and the paper cars that had burned to accompany old Li into the hereafter had just never been delivered to wherever he might be.

Finally I got out of bed, putting on tropic shorts I had taken to France and never worn there. In order to fully appreciate nature's nightly relief from heat I didn't look for a shirt, which was a big mistake. Those mosquitoes met me in the sunroom and followed me out into the semi-dark, shouting for all their relatives to come and join the party. As I walked, smacking at naked parts, it occurred to me that it might be someone's big laugh if, on this hopefully brief visit to the new Malaysia, I got malaria after having avoided getting it during all those earlier years spent in the country. Batim Salong would certainly appreciate the splendid irony of that.

The best thing I had found so far to say about the Pindong

Hotel was that the guest-houses were widely spaced out, as well as being screened by semi-controlled secondary jungle growth, which made for sound insulation as well as privacy. Wild parties in one of those *ofuro* rooms really oughtn't to greatly disturb the other guests.

In filtered moonlight I couldn't see just how much of the Trengannu coastline the hotel had claimed for its settlement, but the area was certainly sizeable, criss-crossed by a maze of sanded paths, which meant that if you lost your way and accidentally found yourself on the porch of a chalet being rented by a glamorous blonde fresh from a Reno divorce, you had a moderately credible excuse handy which she could believe, or not. Screams would probably be heard all right.

I reached the beach area without running into any other insomniac. Here there were no casuarina trees and no undergrowth, just the occasional palm carefully preserved as decoration. Most of the mosquitoes, unnerved by a breeze that could turn cool at any minute, gave up the chase and left. Strong moonlight made it plain why everyone moved down here in the daytime. This was where it all, or most of it, happened. When you came dripping out of the sea, or merely sat up slightly on your recliner, living was just one long barbecue, with booze service as well. Here were vast shade umbrellas supported by old palm stumps and roofed with jungle leaves. Stored under more of these attap-roofed shelters was all the sea gymnasium paraphernalia, water-skis, surfboards, sailboards, pedal boats with love-seats, and assorted canoes. There were also life-preservers for any guests who might have taken the playthings too seriously and been overcome by heatstroke a hundred yards out from the beach.

Apparently there was no risk at all to the expensive equipment from the locals who might have come sneaking in, probably because none of them would have much use for canoes or sea-going love-seats, and it looked as though vandalism for its own sake hadn't yet reached these parts. The bar, though, had been built like a small fort, heavily shuttered, and sealed with stout padlocks. From its size it was pretty obvious that it was well stocked and waiting for a just post 7.0 a.m. re-opening, then probably featuring as a pick-me-up the Pindong Hotel speciality of palm toddy with the gut-rot effect slightly diluted by fresh pineapple juice.

The beach was just a beach, with good firm yellow sand and offering no special tourist features beyond a steel scaffolding tower from which a lifeguard could megaphone a shark warning. I walked along just a few feet from the edge of a gently retreating tide, waiting for the temperature drop which seemed to be falling behind schedule. Perhaps global climate change had rubbed out that old natural relief, leaving nothing but the air-conditioning you have to pay for.

At night the water temperature would be lower than the air, and I considered just dropping my shorts and walking in, not worrying about sharks or the outsize stinging jellyfish that can be a feature of this coast. A long way out from shore there was the flash of what I thought was a fish jumping. The flash came again, no fish, a human arm. I saw a head, capped as for water polo. Then a moon-blanched face appeared for the brief sucking in of air.

Some idiot was out there showing off to himself, that major hazard to those who try to earn a living catering for human playtime. All that was needed to make this hotel's name practically unforgettable to potential customers was a story in the *Straits Times*, plus the Chinese press, about one of our guests losing a leg, or maybe a lot more, to a night-cruising man-eater.

The swimmer was too far out to hear shouts and

anyway that cap meant protective earflaps held in place by a strap under the chin. The noise he was making was covered by the sea's rumble, and if the man had just disappeared, it could have all been imagination made over-ripe by a hot climate causing me to see things that weren't there. But, like the one of that old woman peering in at me from the sunroom, this hallucination didn't go away either. The swimmer went on swimming fast, leaving a wake that could well be setting up a phosphorescence visible from the sky.

Then I saw a kimono. It was cotton, with blue flowers on white, a standard mass product once turned out in Osaka for the world, but now manufactured in South East Asia by much cheaper than Japanese labour. I heard splashing and looked out to sea again.

As if in telepathic receipt of a message from me, the swimmer was coming in towards the beach with a final exhibitionist turn of speed that could be because he had spotted a watcher and could never resist putting on an act for an audience. The crawl was maintained right into the shallows, and then he stood.

Only it wasn't a he. The cap was all she was wearing, no respect at all for increasingly fundamentalist feelings in a Muslim country, not even a bikini strip. She stared at me. In the moonlight her body glistened with the kind of whiteness you rarely see in the tropics, or at least not in the tourist areas.

'Go away!' she yelled.

From her tone I gathered that the final spurt to the sand had not been for an audience. She didn't want me to wade in with the kimono. She issued those basic instructions once again and her voice told me something that my eyes might have picked up earlier if I hadn't been so dazzled by a wonderful whiteness. It was Miss McCollom.

I turned, walking north up the beach, even clasping my

hands behind my back like a contemplative monastic during the recess from devotions hour. Then, having given her
time to wrap herself in cotton, I turned, half-expecting to
see her running past the bar towards the main block. But
she wasn't. She was standing watching the bogus monk. I
walked back down the beach.

'Do you do this often?' I asked.

She took off the bathing cap with one hand and held the
kimono shut with the other.

'Nearly every night. When it isn't raining.'

She then did the getting water out of her ears act,
jumping on one foot and shaking her head, thumping
first one ear with the hand holding the cap, then the
other. I asked if I was the biggest crowd she had ever
attracted.

'Well, I've never heard any applause, Mr Harris.'

'It's a good thing for you the sharks around here don't
go for white meat. They're not used to it.'

'Is that meant to be a warning?'

'Yes.'

'In the time I've been here we've only had three shark
alarms and one of them was false.'

'With all the daytime disturbance I'm not surprised to
hear it,' I said. 'Maybe one of the sharks bit on a pedal
boat. But doing this at night alone is crazy.'

'When else can I do it with my skin? I just don't go pink
in the sun, I turn a sort of purple. Not the kind of girl
you'd like to see behind reception. Or playing the gracious
hostess. And it also hurts. I get blisters.'

'It's not your sort of climate.'

'I know. But I'm stuck with it. So I swim at night.
There's never been a hint of a shark. I think that after dark
they go down to the bottom to sleep.'

'I don't.'

We made the contact practically social, walking up

together through the barbecue area. As we were passing the locked bar I asked an appropriate question.

'Do you have much trouble with the boozers?'

'Not really. Oriental men almost never drink like that. Their wives won't let them.'

'What about their girlfriends?'

'They won't let them either.'

'And those from Western civilizations?'

'We're not tied into any European package deals. Or from the States. Which means you pay a lot of money to get here before you pay our bill. An unconscious husband is a waste of cash outlay.'

She seemed to have got over nerves. I asked: 'Do you get any of those boozing British wild boys?'

'Not so far. They all seem to be doing it nearer home. Or in Bangkok.'

We walked on one of the sandy paths. The increasing breeze had started the casuarinas whispering. For someone who had begun this contact stark naked her composure now was impressive. She asked: 'You don't like what you've seen so far, do you, Mr Harris?'

'Not a lot.'

'You sent back your steak?'

'I hope you have a doggy bin. I don't want to recognize it in the chef's special.'

After a moment she said: 'You can inspect the kitchens tomorrow. That's the sort of thing you came for, isn't it?'

'I came to Malaysia in answer to a cry for help.'

'Oh.'

Her disinterest was put over well.

'The cry for help was from a woman,' I said. 'Presumably Chinese. I think she said she was Mrs Li, but I'm not sure. It was a bad line and she was yelling.'

Miss McCollom had no comment on that. Though I already suspected that she did not, I asked if Mrs Li lived in the hotel compound, to be told that the Li homestead was a mile north on the road to Dungun. It was the estate house in a rubber plantation which the Lis has bought to live in while they supervised the building of the Pindong Hotel. The rubber trees were no longer being tapped and the small hamlet which had once housed the estate workers had now been turned into accommodation for hotel staff. I wondered if the Japanese architect, using my money, had also been turned loose on a conversion of the Li family home, but Miss McCollom couldn't tell me anything about that because she had never even seen the place from the outside. It would seem that Mrs Li had never had anyone to tea even before her husband was arrested, at least anyone from the hotel, the only exception being a certain Mrs Kwing on the staff here whom I had yet to meet. There was more than a hint, from the tone in which that name was served up to me, that Mrs Kwing and the hotel's acting manageress had somehow failed to develop a happy working relationship.

'You never see Mrs Li at all?'

'No. There would be no point in her coming here. She speaks only Cantonese, no Malay at all. And just a few words of English. Li never took her anywhere, except Kuantan sometimes. Typical Chinese homebody.'

That sounded a shade sour.

'Any children?'

'Two. Li used to bring them here sometimes. Both utterly spoiled. And then there's Granny. Mrs Li's mother. She came down from Hong Kong for the birth of her first grandchild. And just stayed. She uses a tricycle to get about.'

'Granny does?'

'That's right. It's quite something to see, Mr Harris.'

'Don't the Lis have a car?'

'The KL police took it to pieces, looking for cocaine. I don't think they put it together again. It wouldn't be any use if they had. Mrs Li doesn't drive. These days she doesn't come out of the house. Granny does the shopping, usually by tricycle, at the little village you passed coming here.'

'Doesn't the old lady ever look in here for a cup of tea on her way home?'

'Not to my knowledge, Mr Harris. Any more questions?'

'I tried to ring the Lis from KL but there was no listing of their number.'

'That's because they haven't got one. There was only an extension to the house from the hotel exchange. The day after Li was arrested the extension line went dead. I suspect that old Granny went out and chopped it through with a hatchet at their end. The mosquitoes are getting at me rather badly, Mr Harris. I'm going in. Good night. And sleep well.'

CHAPTER 7

In my business life I have never really properly understood what my accountants were trying to tell me, and usually I acted on intuition rather than their advice, with moderately successful results. But I needed more than intuition to pull facts out of the numerical and verbal junk heap of the Pindong Hotel's allegedly straightforward history of its own relatively short past. After two hours of working at it I more or less gave up for the time being, falling back on intuition again, this telling me that there was a cover-up somewhere and, even though I couldn't find it, policy ought to have me pretending to be uncovering the full picture.

In those two hours of struggle I had managed to isolate just a couple of positives. One, this place had not at any time since the opening approached fifty per cent occupancy, and two, stemming directly from the occupancy factor, the whole project was simply not a paying proposition and never had been. My investment was suffering from the general malaise which has hit tourism both in Malaysia and Singapore, this the result of an excess of hotel facilities over people coming into the country to use them. Only in Thailand are the South-East Asia tourist pickings still rich, but this could ease off there, too, if many more visitors got shot up by bandits.

I made a memo for future promotional material to state that the Malaysian bandits, who for long wore the label of Communist freedom fighters, have now all surrendered, leaving the country as safe to travel through as Southern California, perhaps even safer. It was a good selling line. I used to do the advertising copy for my own shipping company which had two vessels with six cabins each that I liked to keep as full as possible, the happy passengers being the jam on our cargo bread-and-butter. I know that in my Singapore office they used to laugh at my ads; nevertheless these brought in the paying customers, for it certainly wasn't the food, not on my ships.

The right promotion just might also see an occupancy rate surging up here, in spite of the Pindong cuisine. I looked down at the barbecue which had opened while I continued with my research up in a second-floor room in the central admin block, this reached by a spiral stair from a hall just behind the cave reception area. The office had a huge window which allowed anyone working in this place to more or less oversee the barbecue at the same time, which was probably why Miss McCollom's desk, which I was using, was right up against the glass. It was an efficient-looking desk, equipped with two telephones, and the kind of computer that these days you have to buy the kids to do their homework on, also useful if you need to claim that you have punched the wrong button by mistake and have come up with a total memory chip loss of all your records.

I wasn't using the screen at all, just ledgers plus guest registration books. In one of these I was interested to find that Mr and Mrs Chi Wok Tee, now sharing a page with Paul Harris, had also signed in on other pages at least three times in an eighteen-month period. It was the sort of thing my accountants would never have noticed, but gave me the feeling that it all just might mean a little something more than that we were somehow managing to really please at least a couple of our guests.

Miss McCollom, whom I now called Josie at her own suggestion, was not helping me with my researches. The sound of an electric typewriter hard at it beyond a thin partition came from someone I had been introduced to as our secretary-general. I don't know how she had come by that title, but without a doubt it suited her. This was Mrs Kwing, who apparently had no usable first name. She had risen to greet me rather in the manner of a lady politician who has an enormously heavy schedule but still has to remember that it is the smile which gets the votes.

I got the smile and damn little else, in spite of Josie's assurance before she left us that Mrs Kwing could put me inside any picture she was called upon to display. I hadn't been in that office for ten minutes before I realized that Mrs Kwing had been born with that God-given gift for obstruction which can be so useful in all civil services. She offered me total incomprehension along with pity for my stubborn pursuit of the unnecessary. Her favourite expression, in careful English just tinged with Chinese sing-song, seemed to be: 'Afraid I not with you, Mr Harris.'

Mrs Kwing had apparently been with the Pindong project since the start, specially imported from Hong Kong for the job. She was considerably taller than one expects a Chinese woman to be, and thin with the kind of thinness that looks fringe anorexic but can still be a front for a huge appetite, this possibly tapeworm dictated. It was her face which said she could eat a lot, far too round and plump for the rest of her, and much too positively framed by a squared-off, little-girl haircut. The big feature on Mrs Kwing's face was artificial, a pair of those huge, completely circular spectacles which, by putting a heavy emphasis on the loved one's enlarged pores, have probably helped a lot towards world population control.

I tried to establish an aura of courtesy around myself by getting up whenever I had a question to put to the Secretary-General, going to stand in the open doorway between our two cubicles, usually holding a ledger in one hand with the forefinger of the other hand pointing to some item which I found more than slightly curious, like the Wi Wi Kai Brothers Conglomerate which seemed to have swallowed up all the directors who had been on the Pindong Hotel board when I put in my money. Surely they all couldn't have followed old Li into death? I remembered at least three of their names and had lunched with one of them at least a couple of times down in Singapore. I recited these names to Mrs Kwing but got no reaction at all, so I went on to ask how many Wi Wi Kai Brothers there were in that conglomerate. She didn't know.

'Well, are they Hong Kong or Singapore operators?'

'Maybe both, Mr Harris.'

She was anxious to get on with her typing. She stared at the sheet on the roller.

'Mrs Kwing, have you been with this company since it was formed?'

'Yes, Mr Harris. At first, before hotel building, is at office in Kuala Lumpur.'

'Then that must mean you were around for the first audit?' And all subsequent audits. I'd have thought close enough to get a feel for the general drift of how things were going.

'So why, Mr Harris?'

'The why is simple, Mrs Kwing. For some years as an investor I had no return on my capital. One expects that with a new company. Then I began to get a small income. This improved modestly over the years. And usually when a company is operating at a steady loss the investors get a zero return.'

'I not with you, Mr Harris.'

I was dead certain she *was* with me, all the way, but I went on with a careful kindergarten explanation, pointing out that in order to keep the Pindong project operating as well as sending me that income to France, there had to be a steady pumping in of new capital from somewhere. And that this must have gone on for years when the obvious commercial answer was liquidation. Could it be, I wondered, that those cheques to me had been something in the nature of hush money to keep me from thinking about investigating a business operation?

The Secretary-General took a moment's break from polite attention to me to adjust something on her typewriter. Then she said:

'I do not know of such money to you, Mr Harris. I not treasurer of company, also.'

'Who is?'

'He not here.'

'Where is he?'

'At Hong Kong.'

'Is that where you contact the Treasurer when this becomes necessary?'

She nodded.

'What is the Treasurer's name?' I asked.

She seemed to think about that for rather longer than really ought to be needed when asked to identify a close associate.

'Mr Ching Kwa,' she said.

'Naturally you have his telephone number?'

The lady managed quite a quick turnaround on that one.

'Mr Ching Kwa move office to new place Hong Kong. So I must wait for number change which he tell.'

'I see. Until Mr Ching has been in touch with you from his end you have no way of contacting him?'

'It is so,' she said, almost happily, to her typewriter.

I went back to my desk against the large window once again to sit down after a lost skirmish with Mrs Kwing. I gazed out at the playtime barbecue area. The blue sea was now being marked up by swimmers and a couple of pedal boats. A considerable number of chairs under jungle-leaf umbrellas were occupied, the bar was open, and there was musak from a speaker set up among the coconuts on a palm tree. It might all be some people's idea of heaven, but it wasn't mine.

I went down on a small mission to accidentally make the acquaintance of a Mr and Mrs Chi Wok Tee from Formosa who apparently kept returning to this place for more of the same punishment. I thought about going back first to the Orchid Suite to change into shorts and to leave off my shirt, then decided that I was too pale all over to pass as a dedicated holidaymaker, so I pulled down shirtsleeves, buttoned the cuffs and used the spiral staircase. At reception in the cave foyer was a young girl, Chinese, nubile and extremely pretty. I hadn't seen her before but she must have got some message that there was a man working in the room above who was up to no good. She sent me a look that could be classified as half-frightened. I offered a pleasant smile for her nerves but only got back a professional showing of teeth with no warmth in it.

There was plenty of warmth outside. Just past the midday peak when they ought at least to be seeking shade and contemplating a post-luncheon siesta none of these big spenders looked as they had any thoughts about sleeping through what they had paid for. They were here to be entertained non-stop by a series of memorable Far East experiences which could be carefully memory-banked for reissue when they got home against neighbours who had only been able to afford an economy week in Majorca.

Josie was hostess, which is considerably harder to work at in the mornings than at other times of day. She was wearing a very wide-brimmed hat to protect delicate skin and a button-through dress with a longish full skirt and sleeves. She appeared cool and competent, but somehow less pretty than in the early hours of the morning wearing only a bathing cap.

I had a look around at the customers. In spite of the pop beat coming down from a palm tree Pindong was still waiting to be discovered by well-heeled teenagers, or even by those ageing into their thirties. What we had was a not too exciting selection of fifty-pluses, doing what they hadn't been able to do before their husbands made any money, but still not certain that what was happening to them now was the thing they had dreamed about over hot cookers or in rush-hour commuting. There seemed also to be a painful shortage of rich Americans.

Josie was moving towards me, wearing an expression which said that my coming out to mix with our paying guests was something of a mistake.

'Well,' she said, keeping her voice down. 'What have you found out about us?'

I didn't care for that, so I told her the truth, which was that in terms of any kind of economic reality this place should be shut down, with all the staff made an unemployment statistic.

Her eyes widened. They weren't the usual pale blue eyes of the redhead, more green, and she had felt that they needed the setting of dark eyelashes, these probably dyed to save her having to make them up every morning after her swim. She might have spent her youth conscious that the general effect of her face wasn't positive enough, and the moment she was free from parental control had set about correcting this. The correction was effective. There was nothing at all pale about the look approaching hatred beamed at me.

'Have you come out here to tell our customers that they've got to pack and leave?'

'I'm not a director,' I said. 'Though I might go to a board meeting if anyone around here could tell me where that was likely to take place. But I wouldn't be allowed to vote.'

'Does that mean we can go on breathing?'

'For the time being.'

'Oh, thank you, Mr Harris.'

'That's all right. And now that we are seeing so much of each other hadn't you better call me Paul? Tell me, are Mr and Mrs Chi Wok Tee out here anywhere?'

She didn't have to turn her head to have a look.

'No. They could be in their suite.'

'How do I get to it?'

There was a pause.

'I've just remembered. They went off in their car this morning.'

'Maybe you could introduce me at dinner tonight? I see the bar's open. Can I buy you a drink?'

'I never use it when I'm on duty, Paul. It tends to make my smile seem a little artificial. Why don't you have a swim before lunch?'

She was wishing me a sudden cramp in both knees just as a shark which didn't mind white meat closed in. I didn't go for a swim. I didn't stay for the barbecue either, finding laughing boy Chong just coming out of the Orchid Suite, apparently having been dilatory about making my bed. I told him I would lunch in my sunroom, taking whatever the chef had done to chicken.

'Only beach eatings lunch-time, Mr Harris.'

'I'm having my eatings here. Chicken!'

'OK. I do.'

Pindong went quiet that early afternoon, no joyous shouts from the water, just sun-inflamed skin on prostrate bodies in the process of getting redder. Someone had switched off the palm tree loudspeaker. I saw not a soul on my way through the hotel grounds to the monkeyless parking area with the highway beyond it. It was the time of day about which Noël Coward left that warning.

It was my plan to arrive where I was going during the deep stillness of the hours when even insects tend to give up activity in favour of leaf shade. I had at least a mile to go and was sweating before I had covered even a quarter of that distance, this on a tarmac surface which had patches of sun blister and was hot to the feet. A snake, small and green, was curled up in a drainage ditch, with its eyes shut, but I didn't think it was dead.

The jungle had been slashed open by the road and after years still resented this, huge hardwoods pressing in from both sides. Thick undergrowth insulated out any sound of the sea. Stillness was so intense it seemed almost desperate for the relief of any noise like the rattling of a truck coming up behind me, or a bird call from the top of a tree. Sweat got in my eyes, leaving them stinging. The handkerchief I used to mop my face went back in my pocket a wet ball. I might have been walking through a world already overheating for the great burn-up.

Then I wasn't alone on the road. I hadn't noticed a bend ahead. Someone was coming towards me on a tricycle, a small body held high above big wheels. The rider was dressed in black, defying sun by the colour it most hates, black legs pumping the pedals quite slowly, but without any suggestion of great effort. The machine was heavy, lumbering, but there was no hiss of tyres or rattle from the frame. I heard the rider's breathing, quite loud, synchronized to the rise and fall of black knees.

It was the lady who had watched me come out of my bath. The jade pin was still in place, riveted into a coil of black hair. She rode with her head held up, chin lifted. I rated a brief glance. I don't know what I had been expecting, maybe a half-smile. I didn't get it.

I stood watching her go, almost willing the woman to indulge curiosity by at least one quick turn of her head. She didn't honour me with that much interest.

CHAPTER 8

Most Malaysian Chinese have a peasant ancestry leading back to Hainan Island or the farming area around Canton, but they still seem to me as much an urban people as New Yorkers. It's not just that they dislike the country as such, they are simply scared to death of it. When forced to live out in the wilds to grow rubber or mine tin they don't build themselves ordinary estate houses, but places fortified against the surrounding menaces, these probably including an assortment of devils imported from the old motherland, horned and maybe wearing a couple of tails as well. Not for the Chinese the gracious plantation bungalow with wide-open verandahs and wide-open rooms through which the breezes can blow. The breezes are kept out because awful things can use them as a conveyor-belt to get in at you.

The solid, almost windowless construction of the Li residence was no surprise, though its situation was. The best defensive sites are on high ground, but this house was down in a hollow from which there was nothing like a long-distance view of anyone approaching, the choice of position perhaps dictated by the idea that the safest home is one that nobody is likely to suspect is there at all. Certainly the approach to the place was vague enough, no more than a track scarcely parting the rubber trees flanking it. Even as a pedestrian on the tarred highway I think I might well have missed a disguised drive if it hadn't been for a creosoted mailbox nailed to one of the trees. The box had no name or number, just a padlock not yet suffering from tropic rust. If four-wheeled vehicles sometimes came this way the hard packed clay showed no tyre tracks, and I was a good fifty yards into the rubber forest before I came on what I was looking for. A dip in the track still held dampness from night rain and on the edge of this were clear marks that could only have been made by a tricycle.

I had been very hot out on the tarred road under full sun but was even hotter in the shade, the trees making extortionate demands on the available oxygen. I began to pant on a gradient. From the top of the rise I saw the Li house. Except for slit windows, and few of these, the outer walls had only one serious break in them, an iron-barred gateway into what was probably a flagged courtyard. The whole building, and there was a lot of it, had been plaster-washed a vivid blue, this now time-marred by peeling patches and fungal attack. With the Chinese feel for really garish colour contrasts, the blue walls were topped off by bright green tile roofs at assorted levels. Sticking up from the tiles, like a submarine conning-tower emerging from waves, was a roundish turret with a flat top. I could make out an access hatch on the platform, which meant that a breeze addict could get away up there from a permanent hot stillness in the many rooms below. The man who had built the house might have needed that tower as a place from which he could watch his rubber trees grow, more branches and more foliage every year, which meant a collateral swelling in his bank account.

There are few growing things on what used to be God's good earth more boring than a rubber forest. A pineapple plantation runs it a fair second, but rubber stays right out in front. It is not just the regimentation, endless rows of cloned trees going up and down over huge areas once owned by jungle, but the trees themselves never seem to achieve a time of new green, always dirty brown-grey trunks lifting disciplined branches to bear a crop of leaves that were old before they unfolded. This wood didn't have the usual slight compensation of a weeded tidiness at ground level, the tapping for rubber having been long abandoned, with the jungle sneaking back via sturdy secondary growth.

The house I stood looking at would have turned me into a manic depressive after a forty-eight-hour stay. It was the sort of place about which it would have been quite impossible to find even a small politeness for your hostess. There didn't seem to be anything remotely like a garden outside those blue walls, just a bowing back of more rubber trees to allow the necessary space. I couldn't imagine, either, gracious salons beneath those green tiles, much more likely numberless small rooms with tiny windows set above breathless courtyards. I remembered old Li's rococo plaster palace in Johore Bahru which he had been obliged to mortgage once or twice but had never abandoned, with its tiled swimming pool and general feel of money spilled out over everything. I couldn't see the old man living in this monstrosity even as a temporary base while the Pindong project was under development. It didn't seem a likely setting for young Li either, certainly not the youth I remembered from France who had seemed set right on schedule to become a playboy of the eastern world.

I went on down the track expecting at any moment to hear the baying of guard dogs, but there wasn't a sound, not even squawking from the usual scrawny hens whose meat is all muscle developed from escaping predators. The silence of the rubber forest was almost menacing, though I knew perfectly well that wild life from the jungle rarely makes use of these man-developed areas; black panthers and the occasional tiger in transit, perhaps, and snakes seem to like it all right, but monkeys and birds don't. There is no food for them in those disciplined rows and the trees are too small for the wild, leaping games that simians enjoy.

When I was down on a level with the house I noticed something very contemporary. Flanking the barred gate, and quite high on the wall above it, were two heavily glazed lights that at night would be able to throw strong beams up the track. There were more of these lights at corners of the building. With half my friends in France equipped with anti-burglar illuminations I wasn't too surprised to find the idea catching on in Malaysia; the surprise lay in the fact that I had seen nothing to suggest that grid power from a line along the highway had been brought to this house via poles or a cable tacked on to the trunks of rubber trees. Josie had said that the phone had been cut, which meant a line leading off somewhere through the rubber, but there was no sign of that either. Unless the estate house had its own diesel plant, which seemed improbable with the grid so near, then cables and wires must be trenched under-ground, an expensive business unlikely to have been undertaken for aesthetic reasons, suggesting instead that the Lis were deeply privacy conscious, even the letterbox very inconspicuous.

The arched, barred gate had no bellpush, just a rope hanging beside it, which I pulled. There was a monastic clanging somewhere in the courtyard, followed by silence. After a moment or two I began to get the feeling, no novel experience in our time, of being under surveillance from some kind of electronic eye. I went close to the bars, peering in, but didn't touch them in case they were live.

It was very hot and very still. In the woods a dead branch

fell from a rubber tree, a sharp crack. Another sound, very small, had me looking through the bars again. I was being stared at from just beyond the left-hand margin of my view by a female child. It is hard to pin ages on Chinese young but I estimated about five years for this one. She was out-growing a white dress or it had shrunk in the wash, giving a considerable display of slightly bow legs. She was not pretty and seemed to have been made aware of this already, more than a hint of aggression in that stare. What I had heard was her shoe being scuffed on paving, almost a paw-ing. She did it again. In one hand she held a red ice-lollipop that must have been recently taken from deep freeze but was already dripping, leaving a stain on the white dress. Still watching me, she lifted the lollipop and put it in a mouth which stretched quite easily to take the whole thing. Her jaws started to move, crunching.

When I felt we had stared at each other for long enough I said in Malay that I had come to see Mrs Li whom I did not suggest was her mother, though this seemed likely. There was no sign of message received and understood, and certainly no polite reply to it. She did take out the lollipop and stood letting what little was left dissolve away in heat, as though it hadn't been one of her favourite flavours. Then there was the sharp explosion into English of one word:

'Go!'

A linguist at such an early age. I said again that I had come to see Mrs Li, and the little girl repeated the one word, even louder this time. I did the only thing then that seemed sensible, reached for the rope and really rang that courtyard bell. The girl dropped her lolly stick, swivelled around on the paving, and disappeared.

It wasn't her mother who came out next, just a little dog, late on duty but making a great bluster of yapping to cover that up. It was a Pekinese, the beloved mini-lion, which will attack an Alsatian if this becomes necessary. I was

charged by a dog intending to come straight through the
lower bars, which suddenly realized a few feet from them
that it was a bit wide in the beam for that act. The Pekinese
paused to reassess tactics, stopping the yaps meantime. I
leaned forward and said gently:

'Hi ya.'

If it is true that a dog always knows a good man when
he sees one then I accept the accolade. The Peke seemed
astonished. His head came up, goggle eyes staring. Slowly
the plume of tail rose and began to flip back and forth. We
were having a private conversation when this was interrupted by something like a screech.

A lady was now in the courtyard, about the right age to
be lollipop's mother. She had black hair chopped off just
above shoulder level and fringed just above eyebrows.
Matrimony had seen her putting on weight, moving her
quite a long way towards being actually heavy, and the
attendant stresses had also seen her becoming careless
about appearance, a flowered dress not much more than a
mother hubbard, legs bare, feet thrust into flip-flops. The
screech became a word, the one I had heard from the
daughter.

'Go!'

There was a sucking in of breath, then an addition:

'I no speak! I no speak! Go!'

So I went. The Peke began to bark again, this time on a
note which hinted at sadness. On the track to the main
road I had the thought that I would like to get back to the
Pindong Hotel without meeting an old woman in black on
a tricycle.

CHAPTER 9

I ate with the paying guests that night. The dining-room
didn't carry on the cave motif. In there the decorator's
theme seemed to be aiming towards a third-class Chinese
restaurant, lighting dimmed down by coloured silk
lampshades with tassels hanging out of them which are
almost a certain guarantee that the Canton cuisine will be
fourth-rate. Each table also had its own lamp, pinkish in
tone, this tending to point up the already brightly sunkissed
faces of the non-Eastern diners. On the sea side large
windows had been given the Moorish arch treatment, suggesting that our Japanese architect's creative experience
must have included a ten-day package deal to Spain. The
wall opposite these arches offered a recessed stage, now
curtained off, but clearly meant for late-night entertainment
when the hotel's takings meant that this luxury could be
afforded. I didn't regret that accounts still in the red spared
me the sad spectacle of a team of refugees from Brisbane's
night life on tour of the tropic Orient: half a dozen girls of
uncertain age plus a couple of Australian gag men.

There were two menu cards, one Eastern eating, the
other Western. Apparently you weren't supposed to mix
the two. I had a look at the wine list before deciding, to find
that at some point the management must have bulk-bought
from Tunisia, to which they had attached French prices, so
I went Chinese, advised on this by my waiter who was also
my room boy Chong. I chose what he told me to, probably
what he was eating himself, for at one stage he came
through the swing door from the kitchens using a toothpick.

The meal surprised me: pork given nine different treat-
ments by a real food-lover. It was the kind of dinner which

seemed to account for the fact that more than half the people eating here were Chinese, though the total number of our guests was not impressive. The unused tables had their lights out, and there were a dismal number of these. As a shareholder I wasn't able to take comfort from the thought that many of our guests might be dining somewhere else that evening, for one of the advantages of a hotel in an isolated position is that after a day of sun, sand, booze and sea-going love-seats people just don't have the energy left to get in cars for the drive to the nearest alternative restaurant. In the case of Pindong it meant quite a long drive, either north along the coastal road to Dungun or south to Kuantan. There was no inland alternative, just jungle that way.

Josie didn't eat with us, possibly up in her office controlling the volume of the musak which was entirely half-strangulated Hong Kong pop. The good food should have put me in a happier mood, but somehow it didn't, perhaps on account of too much pork. Someone had turned the air-conditioning low as though in a belated economy bid to keep the Pindong experiment from closing down, which meant that our surroundings were on the warm side. The Westerners were noticing this, the men who had put on jackets for a semi-formal occasion using handkerchiefs to mop themselves, though the Chinese just went on eating steadily, unperturbed by climate. Chong had brought me an iced beer without being asked to, as though he knew I would need it.

I sat in my pink glow suddenly thinking about Li in the Kuala Lumpur jail, seeing again his face across that scrubbed table as he pronounced sentence on himself. What I had minded most then was the sense of hopelessness behind his cry. It hadn't really been an appeal to me, more a lament from a man who saw his fate as settled and a protest against the waiting that was inevitable before the door on life shut. As a people the Chinese can somehow scrape up laughter from almost any circumstance, but a concrete cell had put paid to that relief for Li. I hadn't known him well but I began to feel that I knew him now, there was so little left of what he had been in that shrivelling of his old identity.

I looked up to find that Josie had joined the diners to play hostess again, this time wearing a sun dress she had to wait until after sunset to use. She was moving from table to table to top up coffee cups while behind her came the girl who had looked at me half in fear from behind the reception desk. She was now carrying a kettle for those who were finishing off with green tea. It was quite some time before they reached my table. I was dealt with from the kettle, after which Josie handed the coffee-pot to her assistant, who left us.

'Did you enjoy your meal, Paul?'

'It was excellent. After this I'll eat what Chong tells me to. Won't you sit down?'

She shook her head, but didn't move off. After a moment I asked whether she could point out Mr and Mrs Chi Wok Tee among the dinners. She didn't turn around to have a look.

'They've left,' she said. 'Checked out this afternoon. It must have been when you were off on your walk.' There was quite a pause before she added, 'I hope Mrs Li offered you tea?'

'She didn't let me through the gate. If you have Chong tailing me during the siesta hour I hope he gets paid overtime. Does Mrs Li run slightly to fat?'

Josie's smile was almost warm.

'More than slightly.'

'Then I saw her. And was yelled at. But the dog was friendly.'

'A Peke?'

'Yes.'

'I've wondered about him. He used to be here all the time with Li. I'm glad he's still alive.'

'Why shouldn't he be?'

'Well, he was Li's dog. Those two women might have eaten him. Good night, Paul. I hope you sleep well.'

Whoever may have been at work on the décor, all temporary occupancy rooms look what they are and the Orchid Suite, which had clearly been designed for light relief from serious living, welcomed me with a sneer. The pink orchids had gone into a decline and been removed, but with no replacement. I thought about switching on the *ofuro* and lying in hot water with a long whisky beside me, but that would have come near to accepting the day as a total rout to my interests. I could have gone to the disco which a notice-board in the foyer promised was being put on in the dining-room, and there might have been someone else's wife willing to dance with me if I had asked her politely enough, but I hadn't the heart for the experiment. I lay on the bed staring at a ceiling which really ought to have had a mirror fixed to it. By just lifting an arm to pick up the remote control I could have had television, but I had tried that in KL and got a very old Australian soap badly dubbed into Malay. I had bought two books to read on the plane, giving one up over Greece and the other over the Indian Ocean, knowing I'd never go back to either. So what do you do when you have nothing to do? You go for a walk.

It was too early for Josie to be swimming, but near the lifeguard's tower I came close to falling over a couple of European guests for whom sand had its own imperatives and who were already hard at it, trying, with sound effects, to recapture that twenty-years-ago moment when the world had first stopped for them. I didn't apologize, just pushed off down nearer the water, and I don't think they realized that they'd had company.

The moon was only semi out in contest with a lot of cloud, which made for a leprous effect out on the water, white patches in which something seemed to be stirring up phosphorescence. Then I saw it was a shoal of fish, either surfacing in sportive mood or else about to dive-bomb a shoal of smaller fish beneath them. It was the kind of party which sharks like to join, and I stood for a while watching for a big dorsal fin glinting in a shaft of light from the sky, but the really big fish with the sharpest teeth didn't seem to be surfacing. Maybe they were swimming around near the bottom impatiently waiting for Josie. I found myself wishing she would not do what I had seen her do. A fast crawl is fine, but a hungry shark can move a lot faster. You have to respect the tropics. What surrounds you always, this including a fair percentage of the people, is alien to any gentleness.

I decided to lecture Josie. She might just listen if I made a central theme about how bad it would be for the hotel business to have anything unfortunate happening to her. I could also mention a promotional campaign to save Pindong from the receivers which I was considering starting up, maybe even backing with some of my own money. She was Scots, too, which almost certainly meant that the commercial appeal would be a lot more effective than an emotional one.

The beach was broken by a stream flowing to the sea, the same stream I had been forced to carry my bags across on arrival. Here were stepping-stones meant for use by barefoot customers during the fun hours. They were slippery, but I made it, continuing on down the beach to where a rock outcrop came from among casuarinas, this carrying on for some distance out into the sea, forming a natural wall marking the end to the hotel play area. It is always agreeable to inspect the margins of a property you partially own, and I followed that wall back under the casuarinas.

Walking under the trees even in very patchy light was quite easy, little undergrowth, just a question of pushing aside some of the softly feathered branches, and maybe one-time jungle training kept me from cracking twigs underfoot. At any rate I came silently enough to the edge of the hotel car parking area without apparently alerting a couple in earnest talk by a motorcycle up on its stand. Happy boy Chong Fi struck a match to light his cigarette and then held the flame over to light his companion's so I got her face as well. If this was a romantic relationship it was a slightly surprising one. The lady was Mrs Kwing of the large spectacles.

To be detected as a snooper would be bad for my prestige, so I decided to stand out of earshot just watching. It took about half a minute to decide that this wasn't love or any of its subsidiary attachments, more like a business conference, one of those with the chairman doing all the real talking. In this case it was the chairperson, Mrs Kwing. From the way the glow of her cigarette moved around she was punctuating her points with her hands. Chong Fi might almost have been on the mat.

Then it was over. Mrs Kwing walked smartly towards the bridge leading to the hotel and Chong pushed his bike off its stand. I was expecting him to straddle his machine and kick the starter, shattering the hot peace of the night by an awful clattering from a probably rusted exhaust. But he didn't do this, he walked beside his transport, wheeling it up a steep gradient towards the highway. He must have been well down the road to Kuantan before he started the bike, the sound of this padded by distance. I remembered that Josie had told me that the staff quarters were in the other direction, north towards Dungun.

I decided to have a look to see how the hotel responded to being turned into a nightspot. This took me through the cave foyer which was being used as a recuperation area by disco guests, most of the seats occupied and drinks on the tables. In the dining-room the stage curtains had been drawn back and the recess was occupied by a Chinese disc jockey who somehow gave the impression that he would go anywhere for a minimal fee. I didn't care for the lighting scheme, swirling beams of colour on the thin side, failing to give me the feeling I was about to be made wonderfully happy. A couple of dozen dancers, in spite of variegated lights flashing across their faces, looked sad, out there doing their duty by something they were paying for. The exception was Mrs Kwing. She had been a wild chick in her youth and was now reviving this, her enthusiasm suggesting that she had been at it ever since the disco started up, twisting her body in quite surprising gyrations without apparently the slightest fear of a sudden hernia. Her partner, one of the outsize beach boys who tended to spend their days on a recliner, looked about ready to abandon trying to recapture youth and as if he was now longing to rejoin his wife who was probably already asleep in bed.

The music came suddenly to the kind of dead pause which only a Chinese disc jockey would have permitted. He must have accidentally kicked a switch or punched the wrong button, for the disco beams died away and the central Chinese lanterns, without satellite table lamps, came on, bathing the now motionless dancers in pale pink, which didn't suit them. The revellers tried to fill silence after killer noise with little bits of talk, and some were already shuffling towards the exit when the disc jockey got his switches right and everything started up again, this time with the Chinese lanterns continuing to challenge the jumping colour beams.

Mrs Kwing's old boy left her, almost rudely I thought, and she decided instantly to take me on, advancing with glasses glinting. Seconds earlier, if this had seemed a likely development, I could have got away, but it was too late.

'So, Mr Harris! You also enjoy to lighter side?'

'It's one of my great weaknesses,' I said.

She had a formidable smile, especially when it was tinged pink. I hadn't been offered it before.

'So is dancings?'

'Oh, sure,' I said.

Her beach boy, on his way to the bar, looked back. He didn't say anything, but his message was: Better you than me. Mrs Kwing and I danced. At least she danced, I was the support team. It seemed to go on forever, as though the disc jockey was now suffering a mental blackout and just couldn't decide which buttons to press. When we finally got a reprieve even my partner looked as though she needed a break. I steered her towards the bar. This had a Malaysian treatment pretending to be a palm-thatched hut in a jungle village where all the occupants were alcoholics and kept nothing but bottles on their shelves. I wouldn't have chosen the barman for this particular job. He had a long, lean face bearing a clear record of a history of family troubles coupled to chronic indigestion. But the man seemed efficient enough, and when Mrs Kwing asked for a Tequila he produced a drink that nothing would have induced me to even sip, but the lady seemed pleased.

'You drinks whiskies,' she told me.

'Yes. When I'm not on gin.'

I got one of the flash smiles. When switched on, you half expected to see the top portion of that smile pushing up under the glasses for a share of the magnification. The lady's idea of small talk was aggressive, she threw it at me in hard lumps. She was working towards an assessment of my nuisance potential in this happy community, and I was trying to find out what had brought someone with her obvious tactical skills to a bankrupt hotel on the Malaysian east coast when I would have thought that in Hong Kong she could have exploited her talents to the full.

Neither of us got very far, though I was ready enough to

build up a fairly impressive picture of the big shot I had
been in this country at one time, implying that I could be
again if I wanted to, which she didn't believe and neither
did I. From my side I found out that there had been a Mr
Kwing in Hong Kong, but he was dismissed with a wave
of one hand from which winked the kind of diamond many
a husband has bought to keep peace in the home. But
maybe Mr Kwing's diamond just hadn't been big enough.
Our exchange came to rather a sudden end.

'So,' she said, as if no longer able to control impatience,
'you in Pindong many days?'

'Just as long as I need to be.'

'What mean?'

'It means that I'll be staying until I'm quite convinced
that no one here had a very good reason for wanting Li
Fong Chi out of the way. Murder is a messy business. It
can bring all kinds of complications. Especially in a place
like this. But these days in Malaysia a frame-up leading to
a charge of cocaine-dealing is almost tidier than a bullet at
the base of the skull. And just about as certain. You understand the expression "frame-up"?'

She understood all right. She rose.

'I go now,' she said.

And went.

CHAPTER 10

A verbal bomb thrown at the right time can be highly
effective, but it has its very real risks. And I wasn't at all
sure that I had thrown my bomb at the right time. I walked
back to the Orchid Suite thinking of the risks. It had been
foolish to talk about a bullet at the base of the skull.

I put my key in the outer door. The little foyer was dark

but the main room had the lights glowing. I had put them out. It was too late for room service to be operating even if Chong's departure had meant double duty for someone. The television was on, the sound low but still with some crackling, as though there was thunder in the mountains between us and the transmission point.

I hadn't expected my guest, if I had one, to be lying on the bed, but she was. She was still in the dress worn at the time she was pouring dinner coffee, propped up on pillows and maybe here to see the end of a programme because her own set had gone on the blink.

'Hello,' she said in a quiet voice.

'Hello to you.'

'I know what you're thinking. Well, don't. I came here because I need help.'

'Don't we all?' I suggested.

I sat on the end of the bed, looking at the picture. People were moving on the screen but there didn't seem much purpose in it.

'I've been meaning to lecture you about sharks,' I told her.

'Well, don't do that either. Do you have a cigarette?'

'I don't smoke.'

'Being careful about prolonging your life?'

'That's the idea.'

'When were you last in love?'

I turned my head to look at her.

'Paul, what I mean is . . . how long did it last? Did you get over it easily?'

The couple on the screen seemed about to get down to the business I had nearly fallen over earlier on the beach. It looked as though the scriptwriter had run out of other ideas, or dialogue.

'No,' I said.

'No what?'

'No, I didn't get over it so easily.'

'Oh. That's not much use. I was hoping you could tell me something.'

'Like putting a time limit on a specific form of human distress?'

'Something like that.'

'What the hell's the matter?' I asked.

'It's Li. I love him.'

I looked back at the screen, remembering the whizzkid I had seen in France and that reject from living I had seen in the jail.

'When did this start?' I asked.

'Almost at once.'

'You mean when you got here?'

'Yes. Just about.'

'I hope the setting for the big moment wasn't that indoor rockery we call reception?'

'Don't laugh at me!'

'I'm not laughing. I just don't understand why you are telling me all this.'

'There's no one else I can talk to. I'm alone in this place. Li was my protector.'

It was difficult to see either the whizzkid or the prisoner in that role. I got up and went to a chair facing the bed. This seemed to make Josie uncomfortable, she slid off the duvet and went to another chair. We sat with the set between us, like a monitor in a TV studio. I might have been going to interview her, or she me, the situation almost as formal as that, waiting for a red light to come on telling us that we were live and had to start talking. So I did.

'If you're in love with Li I take it you can't believe he was into running cocaine?'

'Of course he wasn't into it! Li couldn't! He wouldn't be part of that filthy game. He's gentle, kind.'

'This place needs money to keep going. He certainly must have known that. Did he talk to you about it?'

'About finance? Not really. And why should he?'

'Business can be part of pillow talk.'

'Well, it wasn't with us!'

The feeling of a television interview had been dissipated. Between the Oriental playboy and the jailbird I had somehow to fit in a picture of Li the lover, staring with sudden magnetism across a hotel lobby as the new employee put down her suitcase; or perhaps it had happened when he was showing her around the first time. It is an old story that I have never quite been able to believe in. That lightning strike of love deserves another label, and certainly has a low durability rating. I became almost polite.

'How can I help you?'

'For one thing you can get me into the jail to see Li.'

'You haven't managed that?'

'I've tried three times. They wouldn't let me past the outer gate. I didn't have the pass you're supposed to get. The police kept referring me to Li's lawyer, but he wouldn't do a thing to help. He takes his orders from those two bitches!'

'Wife and mother-in-law?'

'Yes. And you can add in the Kwing bitch, too. She's in with that pair at the estate house, right up to that scrawny neck of hers. She goes to see them with reports on what's happening here about every second day. The only reason I'm kept on is that those three can't do without me, at least not yet. Imagine Mrs Kwing receiving our guests. She'd empty the place in two weeks. And Li's wife would be useless here. She's a Chinese breeding cow running to fat.'

Josie wasn't the kind of mistress who could ever learn to fit unobtrusively into an Oriental domestic pattern: the lady of her man's relaxed hours playing the lute and wearing tinsel ornaments in her hair, while the official wife got on with maintaining the family tree. Quite a proportion of rich and near-rich Chinese families still maintain these sturdy patterns which were so vital a part of Victorian England's dynamism.

Josie got up and went over to the curtains which had been drawn across the glass wall, apparently to check whether there was any break in them through which we could be observed. The couple on the screen seemed about ready to start talking again, so I found the remote control and switched them off. When Josie turned the broad double bed could have been offering us both that temporary solution to so many man–woman problems. Neither of us was tempted. She went to a side table and, without asking permission, gave herself a double whisky that would go on my bill. Then she moved around, pausing only to sip from her glass.

'Has Li talked to you about me at all?' I asked.

'Yes. Sometimes. After all, he kept going to France specially to see you.'

After perhaps ten seconds of thought I said: 'I find that surprising.'

'Why?'

'Because the only time I saw him in France was when he visited me at Grasse with his father. And that was well before this hotel was built.'

She stared.

'I can't believe that!'

'It's a fact. Whatever his reasons were for being in Europe, he certainly never came to my house to discuss anything. Can you remember anything he said when he got back here about our supposed contact?'

'Well . . . not really. I got the impression he thought of you as a kind of uncle. His father's friend and all that. I mean, that it was natural he should go and see you.'

'How many times did Li go to France since you arrived here?'

She had the answer at once.

'Four.'

Josie finished her whisky and took the glass back to the drinks table. She stood with her back to me, apparently just staring at the wall. Without turning she said, in a low voice: 'They all lie to you. The bastards.'

Then she was facing me.

'I thought Li wouldn't,' she said.

I asked how long he was away on those trips. She had to think about that, looking calm enough as she did this.

'About two to three weeks. Last time it was nearly a month. But he had to go to America. Or so he said.'

She went to a chair and sat, putting her hands together on her knees and leaning forward over them.

'I'm a fool!'

'Josie, what's the matter?'

'Imagine me never thinking of it! *Me!* When we used to do it for them all the time.'

'You used to do what for whom?'

She looked up.

'Husbands. I was an air stewardess. We had a flat fee for posting husbands' cards about the place. Rome, Cairo, Calcutta. To look like he was never in one spot long enough to get up to much while all the time he was screwing his cutie in Paris. Imagine me falling for that! When I knew exactly how the operation works. I did it myself a few times. But I wasn't a real professional. One of the girls I knew had a portable file. Really organized for the job. Cards for posting anywhere on the route, all neatly in their sections. The Customs boys used to laugh and make cracks about our moonlighting. See why I'm a fool, Paul? With Li the thought that he might be doing the postcards home to loved one act never even twitched in my mind. OK, I wear a big label now. What do you think I should have printed on it?'

I didn't offer any suggestions.

'It was Paris where he had his woman. I'm sure of that. He was never in America.'

'You're rushing things, Josie.'

She didn't think so. Her brain was on overtime, producing too fast for any translation into words. If she really had been in love with Li the case building up against him now could be anodyne against pain. I didn't know whether to leave her with the medicine or try to take it away. I could have pointed out that four visits in three years weren't likely to keep any cutie in Paris happy, not even if that cutie happened to be a wife out for an occasional refreshment in a tired marriage.

The news that Li had frequently been in France without bothering to give me a phone call was something I could live with all right. The thought had moved into my mind, to sit there quite firmly, that those trips away from his Pindong base could so easily have been connected with cocaine-marketing. Those drugs found on him by the Malaysian police could have been a plant on an experienced courier-dealer. Boss thugs in the game are quick to deal with one of their operatives who steps out of line; the temptations to do this are real enough, falsification of the street-level price being one of them.

The racing of Josie's brain had come to automatic stop, the tape of her accusations against her lover needing at least a re-wind, but it wasn't getting it. She was now just sitting there, hands in her lap, pretending to herself that she wasn't weeping. I could see that she was. I still had to put my question.

'What was Li supposed to be going to Europe for? To look at hotels?'

'Yes.'

'Did he come back each time full of big ideas?'

'Not really.'

She stood up.

'I shouldn't have come here,' she said.

It was a statement to herself. There wasn't going to be any repeat request that I get her into the jail to see Li. When she was half way to the door I said:

'If you've got any sleeping pills take one. Just one.'

She didn't answer. She was in the shadows of the little foyer when I called out:

'And don't go swimming!'

CHAPTER 11

I was in the middle of an unpleasant dream of travel in a bumping air seat when something woke me. It may have been a noise but, if it was, it didn't come again while I lay keeping breathing slow and steady. If I had turned under a blanket then whatever was going on in the Orchid Suite would have stopped. I had the feeling it was continuing, action made soundless from practised art.

I had a visitor. Nothing vulgar about him, no break-in merchant, but a key-user. Locks are no good any more, the key-user just whispers to them and the double-bolt action slides back. A chain is better, the intruder really has to fight a chain, but a hotel on a remote tropic beach doesn't apparently expect the professional assault on its guests. I had noticed there was no chain.

I didn't think he had come via the sunroom. Security was good on the sliding glass panel to it, nothing on the outer side to ease gently into surrender, a glass cutter necessary, and they make a noise.

There was still no noise from blackness beyond me. I was pretty certain that I had been alerted to my visitor just as he came out into the main room from the foyer passage. In France I sometimes wake up from my snoring, but I was once almost a trained light sleeper, coming back to consciousness without any interruption in breathing rhythm. Malaysia seemed to have brought those special antennae back into operation again. I was glad they had. Abrupt surprises in the dark can include a knife sliding into your chest before there has been the tiniest warning that this is about to happen.

I'd had my warning. Adrenalin started to flow. I could feel heart rate increase, not all of this from fear. Muscles tightened. When I moved it would be to get well clear of the bed. On a mattress you are almost automatically the victim. Kung Fu claims to teach how to deal with this situation, but the formula antidote to it doesn't often work, especially if your defence is from a very soft mattress.

A pencil light came on. The probe wasn't at once towards me, first a white spot on the floor, towards the sunroom glass wall, a desk, then out. I expected it to be looking at me next. It did. Light felt almost like heat on dropped eyelids. I seemed to feel my visitor moving nearer to the bed. I offered the breathing and slightly open mouth of sodden sleep. My acting had to be carried on for seconds while the light watched. I made a slight movement and produced a small grumble of complaint, threatening to snort myself awake. The light went off.

I didn't hear my visitor move away from the bed, the first sound after what must have been half a minute was the faint scrape of a drawer being pulled open at the desk. Then there was another scrape.

I risked looking. Light reflected up from white paper in the drawer showed the blurred silhouette of a man bent over. The beam moved and I saw the side of his head. He had a disciplined, almost military haircut. He lifted my clip file, the only thing in there, out of the drawer, setting this on the desktop and turning over the pages very carefully, with the light close down on the sheets. He took his time, not apparently listening for any breathing changes from the bed, studying with considerable care the notes I had made on the history of the Pindong Hotel project. It wasn't the sort of material a Malaysian burglar was likely to waste time over, but I remembered that even out here now assorted forms of industrial espionage are more lucrative than pinching diamonds. I didn't take time to be flattered that my notes to myself seemed to be worth money to someone else. I was thinking about moving.

I was still thinking about it when my visitor started to photograph with a mini camera. He had dismissed me to the point of going down on his knees for the job, taking the strain off a bent back. The lens shutter didn't click as the man turned over pages. Only once did he switch off that beam, presumably to listen in the dark to any sounds comeing from the bed. I provided the right ones. The light came on again, a shade carelessly directed, and I knew who the man was and in whose service he was operating. What I had to consider then was that people who have been expensively trained to whisper open door locks tend to keep themselves in fine physical shape as part of career maintenance. It was some years since I had been to a gym class.

My leap from the bed couldn't have been graceful, but it did have the element of surprise and near-shock. There was a great deal of noise, which must have been unnerving to a man who had been making so little himself. No footboard on the bed was a help. I think my feet were still off the ground at the moment of impact. Certainly he was only half up from his knees when my weight smacked him hard up against the desk. He didn't cry out. I had no hold on him, which meant he was on his feet in one second flat. The pencil beam from the torch on the floor let him see enough to grab out for my wrists. He got both. I was up against an

extremely muscular body. In a clean fight I was going to
lose fast. I abandoned decency and used the knee trick.
This was effective. My knees are on the bony side. He
yelled. We were unclinched. I could make out his bent-over
body in reverse towards the bathroom door opening.

I knew the layout in there and he didn't. The *ofuro* had
a depth of at least three feet from its cement surrounds on
which you were supposed to use your soap. The bottom of
the bath was also cement. He had stopped moaning but
breathing noises said he was coming for me. I went down
on all fours, at just the right moment. Before he had actually
touched me with outstretched hands I had grabbed his leg
below the knee, then half rose, tipping him back.

I heard his head whack on the bottom of the bath even
over the noise of my own breathing. He didn't seem to be
making any sound at all. I got up, very shaky, groping
towards the light switch.

Batim's chauffeur Mahmud was sprawled out along the
bottom of the bath. I pulled up the lever which shut the
drain plug, then turned on the water. I went into the bedroom for a bathrobe, returning wearing it, leaning on a
door jamb for support, watching Mahmud slowly getting
soaked. I had plenty of time. He wouldn't start to drown
for a least a couple of minutes, it was a big bath.

The man had come to visit me wearing the right gear for
the job, all black. He could have been one of those Japanese
stage hands who are technically invisible even though they
come on in the middle of the action to shift scenery around.
While I watched he opened his eyes. He didn't seem surprised by the water rising all around him. He moved one
leg, then the other, but gently, an experiment which
scarcely rumpled the flow. He looked up at the walls of the
bathroom, then at me. There were no recognition signals
between us.

Mahmud, now getting really wet, didn't suggest an

immediate threat. What I need was a largeish whisky. The aftermath to acute activity of the kind to which my body was no longer accustomed was threatening me with the shakes. I went back into the bedroom, poured a stout measure to keep shaming weakness at bay, drank most of it, then sat on the end of the bed to finish it off. I could just see the steps that would let Mahmud out of the bath. He didn't seem ready yet to use them. By the time he was I had got to my feet again and was watching from the bathroom doorway. Very slowly he climbed up to the cement surround, then sat on it, dripping from all parts. He seemed somehow sad, as though yet once again life had dealt him one of those rotten hands he had come to expect.

'Turn off the water,' I said.

He had to think about that before he managed it, and had to be told also to open the bath drain. The pace of these reactions to orders was very slow. I lost the feeling that this man was a threat to me. I went back into the bedroom to pour more whisky into two glasses, carrying one to Mahmud along the cement surround. He was still sitting in his own puddle.

'Here,' I said.

He looked up, then lifted a hand for the glass.

'Thank you,' he said politely, in English.

As a postscript to violence that was an odd moment. The bathroom offered a small cane chair and I went to sit in it, about ten feet away from Mahmud, watching while he finished his drink and then tried the experiment of feeling for the bump on the back of his head. After a couple of minutes he stood up cautiously, first raising dangling legs, then testing to see if they would take his weight, which they did. He went to a ledge on which was a heap of towels, and wrapped himself in one. He then sat on the ledge, looking down at me.

I said in Malay: 'I've known your employer Batim Salong for a good many years. When something doesn't work out the way he wants it to, somebody pays.'

Mahmud continued to stare at me.

'In this case it will be you,' I added.

He nodded. Inside that towel he had become a still wet thinker. The lead was clearly up to me, so I used it, starting off by citing one or two cases I could recall very clearly in which Batim had used the chopper, not literally as would have some of his ancestors, but with delicate sublety, leaving a man who had believed he was secure in life suddenly in the opposite situation, and this without a flicker of mercy shown then, or later. I could see that there was no need for me to labour this point, Mahmud's thinking was right along with mine.

I decided to use English by way of finding out whether Mahmud had graduated from Kuala Lumpur university as a Batim Salong scholarship student.

'I think your training has been a lot more intensive than just a Singapore Bentley maintenance course,' I said. 'Learned a lot of languages, have you?'

'I speak English, Cantonese, Mandarin, Philipino Spanish. Also Japanese.'

'All that learning still won't save you. Where did you study lock-picking?'

'Hong Kong.'

'Batim's spent a fortune on you. Though I'm surprised he used a Chinese school.'

'The best,' Mahmud said.

After that he told me another life story, this condensed, in sentences short enough to suggest that his head still hurt. The account did not include a wife taking their child back to her native village. I didn't think that Batim would have wanted a husband, even a bad one, on his undercover staff. When Mahmud had finished his new account he didn't ask for any suggestions as to what he should now do with his life, but I told him anyway.

I said there was no need to feel depressed, plenty of well-trained agents had been unmasked by the other side due to some operational slip-up, but had saved themselves from ruin, and probably from being shot, by the simple device of becoming a double operative. It is a slightly tricky role, requiring perhaps just a little more than average intelligence, but many have survived in it for long years, reaching semi-honourable retirement. I told Mahmud I could see a real future for him if he was prepared to work for me as well as for his long-time sponsor. I mentioned I would pay him well.

Even though he was now shivering a little in the air-conditioning I could see he liked that, which suggested that he had long believed Batim hadn't paid him what he was worth. I wouldn't pay him what he thought he was worth, either, but that wasn't something for now.

When you are using a double agent it is well to remember that the man you have bought still won't be offering you all he knows, invariably keeping a portion back, just as he is doing from the party you are contesting. A spy in this role sees himself as a middleman, operating a kind of balancing act, this leaving him the only one totally in the know, and therefore somehow morally still macho. I had to convince Mahmud that loyalty was not really being totally sacrificed by service to me, that in a balancing act of the kind I was suggesting a form of personal integrity can still be maintained. All this was quite heavy going for me as well as for my listener, but by the time we were back in the bedroom and he was wearing a shirt and shorts of mine, he had stopped shivering, now listening to my dubious sermonette with marked attention. I had given him a second whisky.

In a test run of my new role as his control I suggested

that he continue with the job he had been sent here to do, this being getting my personal notes on microfilm. He reacted well, getting up to search for the tiny camera which took some time to locate in a nest of underbed dust. He was still cleaning a minute lens with one of my handkerchiefs when there was a knock on the main door to the suite.

I looked at my watch. Half past three a.m. The knock was much louder the second time. Mahmud was staring at me.

'Get out!' I said.

I pointed towards the curtained side door to the sun-room. He moved fast. It was just as well. He hadn't quite managed into the sunroom when there was the sound of a passkey being turned in the lock at the end of the short foyer passage.

Mrs Kwing wasn't still dressed for the disco, no high heels, no chunky beads, no tinkling bracelets, just her outfit for work at the typewriter, plain, severe, almost military. She was carrying a revolver which was pointed more or less at my stomach.

The soft life in France, and an increasing innocence swelling from that, meant that I hadn't really considered the possibility that the Orchid Suite was bugged.

CHAPTER 12

Even in this violent age not many people who carry guns for use as part of their argument contrive to look as though they kill for pleasure. Mrs Kwing did. She had a fine range for what was in her mind, just about the range of a cobra which had once reared up ahead of me as I was walking through a rubber estate. Whatever is said about snakes in other parts of the world, tropic snakes cultivate aggression

for the sheer fun of it, like football yobbos. I had represented
no threat to that snake, it had a clear getaway in any direction, and it must have watched me coming for some time
before rearing up to perform that unpleasant dance which
involves balancing on a tail. What the snake said was that
if I took one step nearer to have a better look it would come
to me fast.

Mrs Kwing was saying that she liked to be economical
with bullets, one best, two at the outside, but no wild frenzy
of emptying a gun just to make sure that I was dead. She
wouldn't mind at all if it took a little time for me to die,
though she certainly wouldn't be leaving the Orchid Suite
without making quite sure that this was going to happen.
I didn't need intuition to tell me that this lady had previous
experience of killing in the furtherance of her career, and
probably more than one experience. She held that gun like
an old friend's hand.

We could only have been facing each other for seconds, but
it felt a long time. And during it I had a bad attack of that far
from home feeling which really shouldn't have hit me in the
country in which I had spent most of my life.

I can't even guess what happened then in Mrs Kwing's
mind. It could have been that a small rent suddenly
appeared in her intent, this just wide enough to allow in
reason, and reason told her that this was not the time nor
the place in which to kill me. The gun didn't droop, but
she broke that snake's stare to look around the room. Her
voice came almost guttural from a lingering of desire.

'Where is man?'

'Gone,' I said.

She didn't believe me. Her eyes did a search. She decided
that the huge bed came too near the floor to offer anyone
cover. Almost as though dismissing me, she turned and,
with the gun at hip level, went towards the bathroom. I
had put out the light after Mahmud had changed in there.

She put it on. At the edge of the *ofuro* was a sodden pile of the chauffeur's night prowler outfit. I was working on an explanation of how my black pyjamas had got wet when Mrs Kwing came out of the bathroom. She didn't wait to hear my piece or point the gun at me again, just flipped back the curtain, slid open the glass panel and disappeared. I didn't hear the outer sunroom door being opened, so Mahmud must have left it wide as he fled. It was my hope that he had decided this was no night on which to hang around the Pindong Hotel, but had got clean away fast on his transport.

I sat down on the bed, admitting to myself that I needed to. My heart wasn't just beating, it had gone in for exhibitionist somersaults offering the message that the time had come for me to leave this kind of night life to teenagers. But I got up quite soon and went out into the sunroom where the outside door had a key in a lock which I turned, following that up by making certain that the security system on the sliding panel was operational, after which I took a small chair down the foyer passage and jammed it up under the handle of that door for which Mrs Kwing had a passkey. I then padded back to the bed but didn't undress, just pulled up a sheet against air-conditioning chill, switching on the television.

It was Chinese hour from the local station, Kung Fu film put on at a time when all good Malays ought to be sound asleep and so not available for corruption. There was considerable fascination in watching precisely how I should have dealt with Mrs Kwing and her gun if I had only kept up my training in offensive-defence, which unfortunately I hadn't. The film showed me, too, how my wild leap on to Mahmud had been totally unorthodox and badly timed. Kung Fu doesn't go in for foul play, at least not officially, so I was rebuked there, but I hung on to the finish, somewhat put off by the happy ending that seemed like a complete denial of all realism. The station then closed down after a little tune that must also have been manufactured in Hong Kong and, though I kept punching buttons, I couldn't make the screen come alive. I just lay there wanting another whisky, but I'd had enough for one night, and alcohol doesn't sedate your pulse rate, it accelerates it.

I had been dozing when I had to get out of bed to let in my breakfast, which was not brought by Chong Fi. If the new man was a little surprised to have me walking down the foyer passage in front of him carrying a chair he didn't comment, putting down my tray where it ought to go and making no bid for social contact. When I asked in Cantonese whether Chong Fi was off sick he used a word I had heard quite often at Pindong.

'Maybe.'

The coffee helped me a lot. I was almost ready for the phone call which arrived soon after nine, a voice so strange it nearly had me saying wrong number. It could have been coming from one of those old-time Pi Pai Chai girls, a falsetto near the point of breakdown. I was going to end contact when something stopped me, a change of key perhaps, and suddenly I knew it was Mahmud pretending to be what he certainly wasn't. To let him know that I had broken his code I said:

'Oh, it's *you*, Miss Ting!'

I believe he was very happy then that his device had worked, possibly a first practical application of something learned at one of those training courses Batim had paid for. The gibberish went on, with every now and then a stressed word I was to pull out of the surrounding morass and attach to other stressed words for the message. It was reasonably easy to do this, and though he kept squeaking on about our next meeting at a dance palace in Kuala Lumpur, what he was trying to do was arrange a rendezvous.

I told Miss Ting that, alas, I couldn't meet her in Kuala

Lumpur that evening because I didn't have a self-drive car, and also I wanted to visit Kuantan to have a look at a boat which had once belonged to me but now belonged to the Pindong Hotel. I stressed boat a few times until I was sure he got that, after which I thought he rather overdid things, saying that Miss Ting would always be waiting to see me coming through the door of the entertainment palace where she worked. I hung up to prevent him falling over his own success.

Before my hire car to Kuantan arrived, and after I was properly dressed in a Shantung lemon-coloured suit I had taken to France and never worn there, I did a brave thing. I went up to the office Josie had loaned me for my researches. But there was no one about, no Mrs Kwing, no Josie, just the look of a place which has been tidied very carefully, the files I had been using apparently put back into locked cabinets, the electric typewriter hooded with the memo pad beside it naked of any notes. I went down to the cave reception area in which there was only a Chinese woman using a vacuum over some rag rugs that could have been specially woven to match the curtains. I rang the bell on the desk and after some time the pretty girl, whose name no one had given me, came out from a passage to send me a look which said that in spite of my lemon-coloured suit I still reminded her of Dracula. She couldn't help with any news about either Josie or Mrs Kwing. I crossed the lobby with the feeling that the girl's stare never left my back. The woman with the vacuum ducked her head to avoid eye contact. Maybe the suit worried her.

In the hire car I sat having my more than slight hangover bounced by a road which had suffered from overloaded trucks bringing iron ore down from Dungun. Though I didn't want to think, I had to. I wasn't happy about the morning's total wipe-off of any acknowledgement of what had happened the night before. It is unusual to have a senior member of a hotel's administrative staff enter your room by passkey, pointing a gun at your stomach, and then, the next day, being totally unavailable for comment. A disappearance is certainly one way of letting a heated situation cool down to the point where it is safe to touch, but that didn't feel like the right explanation. Much more likely no one was around because everyone who mattered was up at the Li mansion for an emergency breakfast conference.

The meeting might even include Josie. I wasn't by any means convinced that she really hated the people who employed her. It was also worrying to be certain that your accommodation is bugged, this clearly being the explanation for Mrs Kwing's sudden intrusion into my private life. After breakfast I had searched the Orchid Suite and its bathroom very carefully indeed, the job almost reviving old skills, but I had found nothing. This could mean that the necessary mike had been fitted during the construction of the hotel; there might even be a selection of these devices embedded in the fabric, as in the US Moscow Embassy so unwisely built by Russian contract labour. I asked myself if this could have been done with the knowledge of old Li, now in a Chinese heaven, and the answer to that was yes.

The streets of Kuantan were in better condition than the road leading to them. As a boy I had loved this town. Then it had been a long way from anywhere important, seeming three-quarters asleep, especially in the daytime. At night it came awake a little, with *ronggeng* music from crackling loudspeakers, and people in and out of shops, which stayed open. On family holidays I was particularly fascinated by the whorehouse, my questions on the subject somewhat awkwardly parried by my father, which forced me back on my own researches. These were quite comprehensive and revealed that the place was run by a Japanese Mama-san, who was probably also the local spy for Tokyo's Foreign Office. I remember that she seemed very old, possibly even in her forties, had one gold tooth in front, and was always bowing. She employed local talent, most of the girls somewhat sullen-looking. If you were obviously too young to be a client, Mama-san was still very friendly, probably with an eye on the years to come, cracking Far Eastern jokes in broken English and hiding the gold tooth behind one hand as her body rocked with laughter. There was a certain amount of underage drinking of Tiger Beer in her outer salon, which had an earth floor and rickety tables. The girls sat up on a sort of stage and didn't even try to smile at Mama-san's jokes.

I had been expecting change in Kuantan but had hoped for less than there was. The whorehouse was now a boutique selling silk woven sarongs and Kelantan silverwork, and the main street looked as though it had been kept picturesque under police enforced regulations issued by the Malaysian Tourist Board. I didn't go for morning coffee in one of the new hotels, pretty soon making my way down to the river where there was also much change, fishing craft mostly replaced by funboats probably belonging to weekenders from Kuala Lumpur. For my service craft I had built a small dock on the river bank, but this had been extended to the point where it might almost accommodate a cruise liner. Instead of the banana plantation which I had thought of as a suitable place for my emergency conference with Mahmud there was now a car park with the access road to the waterfront leading straight through it. I walked on concrete towards the river looking for my old boat, certain I would recognize it however much it had been tarted up with awnings and glass windbreaks for the pleasure-seekers. A police car came up behind to pass me at some speed, the driver using his horn often. Down on the wharf was an ambulance and another police car. There was also a considerable crowd at one point, though the rest of the dock was deserted.

It had been my plan to locate the boat which had once been the joy of my life, then to walk up and down beside it in quiet mourning for what it had become, allowing Mahmud to work out how to make contact. Some new thinking was indicated. There was going to be no unobtrusive get-together while police cars whizzed about, which meant I had time to kill. I decided to join the crowd. My newly acquired double agent just might be down among those people.

It turned out he was. I came out from behind an ambulance just as a stretcher was being hauled up from a small boat. The strapped-on load had once been human, but wasn't any more. One arm dangled, the fingers of the hand curled in, as though from gripping hard on something. Water dripped off bent fingers, off the arm, and through the stretcher. The crowd was pushing in for a ritual gloating over death choosing someone else. I didn't need a better look. Mahmud would never again have to strain his imagination inventing a new history of himself. And I had now to move away at considerable speed, but with a cautious start.

CHAPTER 13

The hotel phones had those plastic, transparent half-igloos over them which promise a certain privacy, but in fact give none at all. What you can do under one of the hoods is twist about frequently to see whether the world is watching. I was a real squirmer, but had the row to myself, none of the American tourists wanting to phone back to Kansas to find out how the dog was standing up to the loss of his loved ones. Instead everyone was in the bar, needing restoratives after trying on sarongs in the ex-whoreshop. One

part of my twisting brought into visual range a notice-board
offering the local attractions, these including a trip up the
coast in the early hours of the morning to rape the privacy
of giant turtles coming ashore to lay their eggs on a beach.
Or you could go to a blowpipe party in an authentic jungle
tribal village if you were willing to pay the entrance money,
which I wasn't.

To get to Batim this time I had to work my way through
a defence net of three secretaries, two of them male, all
using English and the last one with a bruiser's voice. Then
it was the man himself, still probably out on the lounger by
the pool.

'What do you want, Harris?'

'Mahmud is dead.'

There was silence. Then: 'I don't believe you.'

'Contact the police in Kuantan.'

'When?'

'I can't give you times. I just saw him being fished out.
It'll be death by drowning. All you need for the right
autopsy reaction is to hold the victim under a foot of water.
For some time, and being careful about bruising. Then
you've got an accidental death.'

'How are you in on this?'

'We were to meet. I'd recruited him. You didn't pay him
enough. And I'm not continuing this chat for much longer.
You'll meet me in the Genting Highlands this evening. I'll
be staying in the biggest hotel. Under the assumed name
of Richard P. McPherson. Don't ask me what the "P"
stands for. If they want to see my passport for registration
I'll refer them to you as my oldest friend in Malaysia. At
exactly seven I'll be going out for a pre-dinner stroll on the
road below the hotel terraces. And you'll roll up in your
battle wagon. You must have another man who can drive
that thing?'

'I am *not* meeting you,' Batim said.

'Wait until you've had your lunch. Then, instead of a siesta, do some deep thinking. It'll make you get in the Bentley and come up a mountain.'

I put down the phone. I didn't join the tourists to eat. One thing about carrying cash instead of credit cards is that you can flash it as an immediate inducement to get what you want quickly. I got a year-old Toyota and a driver who used intuition to tell him that there was nothing coming at us on our side of the road around the next bend. On the way up to The Gap we passed a couple of lorries so close there was only a skin of air between us, and both times there was audible shouting from drivers' cabs, this setting up rock-bounced echoes down into the ravines. Normally that drive would have worried me considerably, but the man was doing what I had told him to, and right then a road accident was well down the list of ways that my career could suddenly end. I still retained a vivid picture of Mrs Kwing with the gun held at a businesslike height just above her hip, and with her elbow tucked into her side to cushion any recoil. Out East there are so many exotic ways you can die fast, like eating a prawn curry, or receiving a dart from a blowpipe. I've never used a blowpipe myself, but I'm told that even a beginner can achieve a remarkable degree of accuracy up to thirty yards. And it is so quiet, that total noiselessness almost friendly, just the faintest of phut sounds as you send it off, and with the really skilled operator, not even that.

Kuala Lumpur flaunted its new, towering, semi-bankrupt skyscrapers from a considerable distance, these certainly original in design, possibly a new art form, though personally I prefer the old conventional colonial buildings incorporating the will and spirit of the late Queen Victoria, with just a few Oriental knobs stuck on as trimming. I have a particular weakness for the Anglican cathedrals still be be found scattered across vast areas of what used to be the British Empire, these in tropic Gothic, a challenge to the palm trees all around, stating very clearly that within their walls God will be worshipped in a decent and traditional manner. Such a pity most of them are now cinemas.

I paid off my driver, and with the bonus promised, this in front of what used to be the Government offices with windows staring over a grassy 'padang' at the Selangor Club, that scene of so many splendid Imperial dissipations. The man was sweating, scared by his own driving. He thanked me, but was really applauding his own skills behind a steering-wheel. In early afternoon heat I walked back towards the main shopping area which had suffered less change than the rest of the city, though the skyline beyond it was dominated by banking towers, one of them with curious projections high up, like folded wings, which suggested that it had recently set down rather heavily from outer space.

I had quite a bit of shopping to do, building up the identity of Richard P. McPherson, everything from toothbrush to underpants, plus a floppy case to carry them. I replaced the lemon-coloured suit with one of the well-advertised made in twenty-four hours for the traveller two-pieces. They still measure you to pad out your ego, but the suits are now mass produced in all sizes, ready and waiting. The Chinese salesman started a spiel about how lucky I was because a gentleman of precisely my size had returned my suit as the wrong colour just the day before, and then he stopped, perhaps from something cold he saw in my eye. But it was quite a nice suit, the ultimate in lightweights, a sort of dust colour. I bought a tie to tone in. I still wear them.

You can helicopter up to the Genting Highlands but it remains enough of a novelty still to make the traveller by this method a shade conspicuous, both at take-off and land-

ing, so I hired another car, this time without instructions
to make speed. My new driver fancied himself as a tourist
guide and kept up a boring monologue about points of
interest along our route, most of them decidedly familiar to
me. But I didn't tell him to shut up, staying with my new
identity as Richard P. McPherson, and giving out suitable
little cries of traveller's joy at vistas indicated by a pointing
hand which should have been on the steering-wheel. I found
my mind's eyes switching to other views, in France or Scotland, these totally without a covering of jungle. Those of us
who have spent any time at all in tropic rainforests can
usually get along very well without widening that experience. It's not just the snakes. Under the endless green shade
the thought of death bullies you all the time, and only liars,
or extrovert fools, pretend that it doesn't.

The Genting Highlands have triumphed over rainforest
by peeling it away over the whole of a mountaintop, this to
make room for assorted play palaces including a huge
casino, the idea apparently being that jet-setters are bound
to be getting tired of Las Vegas and about ready to replace
that ageing fun resort with a sanitized peak in South Asia.
But the message doesn't appear to have really got around
as yet, the biggest hotel giving an unbooked feel. They were
pleased enough to see me not to require any documentation
for Richard P. McPherson, and smiles practically pushed
me from registration across the lobby into a lift, and up and
up to the kind of room an unambitious man might hope to
wake up in after death, more solid comfort than flash. I
took a shower in a bathroom which I was pleased to find
didn't have gold taps, and after it went down to the coffee
shop for a snack, deciding that I didn't want a meeting
with Batim on an empty stomach.

I was sure he would join me. Whatever he might have
found out from his Kuantan contacts he would know that
I could tell him a lot more. Also, I would be meeting a man

who would still be angered by Mahmud's having suc-
cumbed to that outstanding tendency of our time, loyalty
sacrificed for more money. A couple of ham sandwiches
would go some way to fortify me against tensions, and I sat
chewing by a window through which I could watch one of
the things I would be paying for up here, the sunset. This
evening's effects were being heightened by a long, black
cloud over the sea's horizon that might have been brushed
in to hide Sumatra. There were also green streaks amid
vast flames of red and near-purple, like special portents
of coming trouble. I had seen that same green before
typhoons.

I had said seven for my meeting with Batim on the road
below the hotel but I stood at the bottom of a long flight of
stone steps for nearly half an hour before a car came slowly
towards me on sidelights so dim they might have been
candles. It was a big car, proud that it made practically no
noise on low engine revs. All around the night was also
silent, no moon yet, not even starlight to show how the
jungle had been pushed back like a cuticle to make improbable an intrusion by supper-hunting panthers. On the way
up my driver had told me that pythons still came sliding
out of the rainforest to lie around on the new tarred roads,
refusing to acknowledge man's takeover.

Batim's reserve chauffeur must have been wearing night
vision glasses, for he stopped his vehicle within three feet
of me and with not the faintest squeak from brakes. It was
only then I saw that the car was not a Bentley but a Mercedes, a slight surprise, for the make's long association with
rich Chinese should have ruled it out for Batim's garage.
Another surprise was no suggestion of chauffeur emerging
to open the door that would allow me in for a rear-seat
conference. Instead an arm must have reached over from
the steering-wheel to open a front door. The courtesy light
had not come on. A voice said in English:

'Get in! Quick!'

It is not the way I like to be addressed by chauffeurs.

'Like hell I will,' I said. 'Who are you?'

'Ming.'

'Whoever you are, Mr Ming, you can drive on.'

'No! Ming Kai Tek! The lawyer!'

'Who have you got in the back seat?'

'No one.'

'Show me.'

A light inside blinked on for just long enough to make it quite plain that there weren't a couple of gunmen back there waiting to be persuaders.

'I don't need a lawyer at this time of night,' I said. 'If it's the casino you want, Mr Ming, just keep bearing to the left.'

'Mr Harris! I am come from Tunku Batim Salong.'

I got in then and shut the door. I was angry. And it was sinister that Batim could afford to stay home, probably eating.

The car moved off. It was automatic, otherwise gears might have crashed, for my host was under real tension. It vibrated off him in etheric waves and there was more than a faint smell of sweat, something you don't often notice among the richer Chinese.

'If you've something to tell me,' I said, 'let's find a place to park.'

'No! I keep driving.'

'We can only go round and round a mountaintop.'

'I do so! I don't stop!'

A moment later I said: 'All along this road are sheer drops to one side. It's a long way down to jungle. And that's no cushion when you get there. Do you have headlights on this thing?'

'Sure. I don't use.'

He seemed to have retained certain positives in his identity, which slightly altered the impression I'd had of him in KL, but not all that much.

'If you're message boy,' I said, 'what's the message?'

'I bring your passport, Mr Harris.'

CHAPTER 14

We didn't stop. Every now and then fun palace lights showed where the road was, but mostly we were under glow-worm illumination. In the course of perhaps half an hour only two cars came at us, one of them honking wildly. Though Mr Ming did seem to know what he was doing most of the time, a very real nervousness about this ride tended to undermine the firm tone of my interrogation. And the lawyer's reactions came mostly in sub-standard English.

'How did you get hold of my passport?'

'Policeman.'

'You mean it was brought to your office?'

'Yes.'

'Why bring it to you?'

'They say I your lawyer. I not like.'

'Then why take it?'

'If police say you do one thing then you must do.'

'Sure,' I said. 'That's democracy.'

'No,' Mr Ming corrected. 'It because I Chinese.'

'Have you had any contact with Batim Salong?'

'Yes. Telephone.'

'His call came soon after you took the passport?'

'Yes.'

'So His Excellency gave you your orders?'

'Yes.'

After a moment or two I said, 'Well, thanks for the passport. Not having one is an unpleasant feeling. How about you and me going somewhere for dinner?'

'No!'

'But after that long drive from KL you must be hungry?'

'I not hungry. I go home. Here is passport. Take!'

I took it.

'Was there no message for me from His Excellency?'

'No. *I* have message, Mr Harris.'

'Yes? What's that?'

'I do not assist in case of Mr Li in Pudu jail. Such matter is finish.'

'So I'll have to be getting my passes to see Li through someone else?'

'I think you don't get pass now, Mr Harris.'

He brought the Mercedes to a gentle stop from a cruise speed of fifteen miles an hour.

'Here is steps for hotel,' he told me. 'When you are in Kuala Lumpur you do not come to my office.'

'So there are to be no meetings of any kind between us?'

'No meetings. Do not telephone.'

'So it's good night?'

'Yes. Good night!'

I opened the door and got out. I looked back into a darkness with no courtesy light.

'I hate to end a relationship like this,' I said.

'Shut door!'

I watched the Mercedes disappear, its tail lights brighter than the ones up front. I had a feeling that Mr Ming wasn't going to switch on full heads until he was well on to the road down the mountain.

They were eating when I got into the hotel, but I didn't feel carefree enough to spend time considering which international cuisine I'd risk indigestion to sample, so I went straight up to my room. In there the lighting and décor said that everything in the world was getting better now and I was free to really relax, but I didn't believe this, and after about ten minutes the phone rang. Batim Salong had a tail on me who had reported in that I was back in the hotel.

'I want you to listen to me carefully, Harris.'

'With you I always do, Batim.'

'There is a helicopter coming down to KL at twenty-one fifty hours. You will be on it. The machine lands at the airport. You will proceed to overseas terminal to pick up the ticket on British Airways flight leaving for London non-stop at twenty-three ten hours. The ticket is under your own name.'

'You're eliminating Richard P. McPherson?'

'I am. Your hotel bill has been dealt with and your air ticket paid for. Tourist.'

'I always fly first these days. My feet swell up in Tourist.'

'Then discomfort will make this trip memorable. You'll have to pay your own fare from Heathrow to your home in France.'

'And what's your postscript to all these travel arrangements, Batim? That I will never again be allowed to set foot in Malaysia?'

'I wouldn't say never. Twenty years, perhaps?'

'By which time, with any luck, you'll expect me to be dead?'

'Let's not put any sinister implications on things. It's just that it has now become advisable you leave this country at once. Arrangements will be made for anything you may have left at your Pindong Hotel to be sent on to you. At our expense.'

'Thanks. What happens if I try to make a run for it? You know, down the mountain. After all, I've been trained in jungle treking.'

'I suspect that you have the wrong shoes with you for anything so ambitious. And I seem to remember that not all of your earlier jungle expeditions were a huge success. No, I think it is best that you stick firmly to my plans for your immediate future. Otherwise there might be an unfortunate accident, leading to expensive hospitalization and unnecessary suffering. Perhaps in your hurry to come out here you forgot about adequate medical insurance?'

I had forgotten. What I said was: 'Next time you are in France, Batim, remember I'm a splendid host. There will always be an open door for you. And bygones will be bygones.'

'So nice to know,' he said. 'But I don't travel much now.'

'Are you saying that contacts will be reduced to cards at the New Year?'

'Spare yourself the trouble,' he told me, then hung up.

I sat wondering whether I would try to ring him back through all those middlemen. My mind felt crowded by the things I ought to have said, but hadn't. If ever a prince needed to be yelled at this one did, but an arrogance inherited from a long line of socially well placed forebears would keep him immune to any shouting from the likes of me. After about ten minutes I gave up brooding and ordered sandwiches from room service.

The waiter who brought them could have been in Batim's service, but probably wasn't. And after he had gone I knew that if I got up to check the corridor I would not see a sinister figure ducking out of sight around a corner, more likely a hotel maid carrying fresh towels ready with that smile for the paying customers. And yet I knew with a certainty that was like the acid in my stomach about to contest those sandwiches that Batim's seeing eye would be on duty for as long as I was in Malaysia.

I packed all that had belonged to Richard P. McPherson into the soft carryall I had bought for his identity, then left a room in which I had only napped on the bed, going down to the main floor in the certain knowledge that everything

would be made pleasantly easy for me provided I showed
no intention of deviating from Batim's careful arrangements. And it was like that, smiles at the reception desk,
everything taken care of, including the slightly mocking
wish that I would be back for a longer stay next time. I
didn't have to order anything, the car to take me to the
mountain helipad was waiting, no money changing hands
at all except for the porter who had carried Mr McPherson's luggage. The boy didn't want to take a tip, but I
insisted on making this obituary offering to my now dead
alias.

The helicopter took off in bright moonlight with five other
passengers, all male, all looking as though they had lost
money they couldn't afford at the casino. There was one
Westerner who might be middle management and was certainly running to fat, who didn't react to my polite nod as
we climbed aboard and so was probably British. Two
Chinese weren't socially inclined either and a couple of
Malays who chattered throughout the flight were maybe
suffering from nerves. I could have worked away at who
was Batim's man in this lot but, since I was doing what I
had been ordered to, identifying my tail didn't seem important. I stared out of the window as we vibrated down from
something like four thousand feet.

Jungle by moonlight from the air looks about as unattrac-
tive as it does by day and there is so much of it. Small
aircraft dropping into that stuff vanish like a fly landing on
the petals of one of those exotic flowers which eat them for
a living. Looking at the tops of those trees, I decided suddenly that the Far East is too complex for anyone over
thirty to live with. Before thirty a certain innocence is your
armour, but after that you've lost it and the scene sours,
becoming a breeding ground for an all-encompassing cyni-
cism. Orientals feel exactly the same way about the Western
world. The two great human divisions on this planet remain

as they have always been, in our time the mutual endurance contest greatly intensified by swiftly increasing economic interdependence.

I got out of the helicopter carrying these dark thoughts and Mr McPherson's travel bag, walking briskly to the checkout counter where, sure enough, were my travel documents in the old name I'd had to live with for long enough. I had no sense of being followed into the men's room or of anyone watching at the bookstall to see what I was going to read on the long, long flight ahead while my feet swelled up. I bought a newspaper, probably the last *Straits Times* I would see, and a book on the subject causing so many people deep concern these days, called *Whither Japan?*. I went to the bar and ordered a double brandy as a sedative for the first hours of the flight, taking the drink to a table where I sampled my book, but got no stirrings of enjoyment. When the flight was called I walked towards it, leaving the *Straits Times* behind, suddenly hit by a strong sense of having made a complete fool of myself by coming East. This was followed by the equally powerful conviction that I wasn't going to be able to duck my ego under a charge of cowardice simply because of the manner in which I was being obliged to leave the Orient. I tried to tell myself that my invisible escorts were somewhere around, and watching, but this didn't improve morale in the slightest. The plain fact was that I was returning to France like a dog after a night on the town coming home with the hope that kind master will just let him get to his bed to sleep the whole thing off.

In the Boeing I had a middle seat in a nest of four. Since you couldn't see out of a window the only thing to do was watch the inflight movie, unless you bandaged your eyes and elected for Beethoven via earphones. Perhaps the stewardess had caught a whiff of my breath as she pointed out where I was to sit, for I simply could not get a message to her about more brandy, the youth on my left having abandoned himself to his Walkman, jigging portions of his body in time with what he was hearing, while on my right were a middle-aged couple who might have been coming back from a month with beloved relations in Australia and were now either snoozing or at prayer. I was left with the choice of *Whither Japan?* or listening to the engines in a bid to find out whether that funny little coughing noise was coming from one of them, or wondering whether the first turbulence would start up just as they served the free food.

Then there was a big surprise. The voice of our temporary God, with a slight Cockney accent, came from the flight deck. We were to make an unscheduled stop at Bangkok to pick up an ailing Briton who, like me, had to get out of Asia fast for health reasons. This caused a real buzz in the cabin, everyone quite excited except the boy with the Walkman who just kept on twitching. In due course news reached the seats in front which just had to be authentic because someone in the queue for the toilets had got it from a stewardess. We were about to pick up a British Vice-Consul suffering from a complete and very sudden mental breakdown as a result of two years in Thailand trying to deal both with the Thais and with hordes of tourists who had lost all their money. The couple from Australia, now awake, were apparently moved by this human tragedy and the lady leaned over her husband towards me to ask: 'Do you think we'll be able to *see* the poor man?'

The landing was a good one, no bumps, and the voice from the flight deck told us the plane would not be motoring up to the terminal buildings, staying out on a reserve runway. After the engine switch-off we heard the sound of the big door up at the foyer to the first class accommodation, then the heavy noise of a truck that must have been pulling the access gangway, followed by some shouting. We had been asked to stay in our seats unless obliged to heed a call of nature, which an interesting number of passengers apparently now found it necessary to do. I went on sitting quietly but quite soon became aware of an almost physical sensation, as though my spine was telling me it was stiffening up. After a couple of minutes of this feeling I had to nudge the Walkman listener to let me past him, which he pulled in long legs to allow. I was then in the aisle, a man with a purpose, which was not the purpose of anyone in the toilet queue. I had to pass waiting passengers to see what I wanted, and a woman's voice said testily:

'Hey, *you*! What do you think you're doing? You just get back there!'

What I had wanted to see was whether the gangway had been pushed up to the plane's open door. It had. A stewardess turned as I stepped out into a white beam of light directed at the steps. She yelled at me.

One of the flight deck crew was at the foot of the gangway, but he was staring at an ambulance from which a stretcher was being lifted. They had strapped down the Vice-Consul in a way which suggested they were expecting him to become violent at any moment. The stewardess shouted again, but the flight officer didn't seem to hear, or didn't turn fast enough, and I was past him, on tarmac, running. Bangkok airport was tinselled with coloured lights as though en fête to offer me a real welcome.

CHAPTER 15

I had never been to the Ponchana Restaurant in Bangkok though I had heard enough about it from Ranya Nivalahannanda, the Senior Vice President of my Hok Lin Shipping Company, when she was down in Singapore helping me to run it. She had owned the eating house before moving south to get away from a divorced husband who still had the legal right, under Thai law, to go on spending the money she earned. It had been a real case for a local women's liberation movement to get their teeth into if there had been one of these, but there wasn't, and anyway Ranya was perfectly capable of fighting her own battles unaided, as she had frequently proved while helping me to fight mine.

I had no difficulty in getting to the restaurant—in Bangkok they'll take your money fast in whatever currency you bring—and I found a taxi soon after getting clear of the runways via a cargo gate someone had carelessly left just slightly open. With any luck Ranya, at only 1.30 a.m., would still be counting the day's takings, and I got out of the taxi with the feeling that it was time the gods served me at least a small dollop of kindness. The driver didn't care for my tip, and when I didn't increase it, he left me with what I guessed—for I don't speak Thai—was the wish that I would soon add my bones to those of my ancestors, and this via a highly painful terminal experience. The tourist trade has killed politeness everywhere.

The restaurant had a neon sign. It was out. In deep shadow underneath was an iron grille over double glass doors. The taxi's rear lights disappeared and the street went quiet, not a residential area, but dedicated to the kind of commerce which doesn't have a shopfront and so is heavily closed down after early evening. If my former Vice President had originally set up here to pick up the executive luncheon business, it looked as though she must be totally missing out on the frenetic night trade. I wouldn't have believed that there was such a near-holy stillness anywhere in Bangkok; there weren't even any pedestrians, just a discontented cat in a lane somewhere.

I took hold of the grille and shook it. That didn't make much noise, the central uprights at the join saying they were tightly nested down in concrete. I began to have the sharpest sense then of the sheer lunacy involved in all sudden gestures against fate like the one which had taken me off that plane. This was probably why I started kicking at the grille. Someone was going to wake up among these night-abandoned tenements of commerce, if it was only a caretaker.

Someone did. A window opened just above the blacked-out neon sign and from it poured a real volume of what I guessed was Thai abuse, whoever was up there, a female, practically making an operatic aria out of it. I stepped back into the road. The window was small, possibly for security reasons, and the head just managing to poke out of it almost invisible.

'Anyone speak English?' I yelled.

The Thai ceased. I heard someone suck in breath as though it was really needed, then the voice called down:

'You English . . . drunk! Go England!'

A lot of restaurants these days, and not just in the Far East, keep that phrase handy for regular use against Britain's world travellers.

'I want to speak to Mrs Nivalahannanda! Does she live here?'

'No speak! Go!'

It looked as though my chances of getting indoors weren't much better than they had been at a blue house in a rubber forest.

'Tell Mrs Nivalahannanda it is Paul Harris! *Paul Harris!*'

'Go!'

It was then I heard the sirens. Throughout the world the police cars seem to use the same sirens. Manufacturing these mechanical screams must be a good business to be in, the market demand not just holding steady, but increasing as more and more of the backward countries become civilized.

The signal to me was clear, and I acted on it at speed, looking for the lane from which the cat had complained and finding it. It was dark and welcoming, resisting even the approaching headlights, not quite opposite the Ponchana but near enough.

The restaurant building was coming alive, suddenly lights in the entrance area, though the neon stayed dark. Tropic damp had got to the police car's brakes. Metal doors banged behind men getting out. The car's full heads went on glaring down the street, law officers don't have to pay for new batteries.

Behind the Ponchana's grille a young woman in rumpled floral pyjamas was working on a lock. It certainly wasn't Ranya. The grille opened wide enough to let two of the policemen inside the entrance recess. Another two stayed outside, turning to look up and down the street as though trying to spot suspicious characters but not suggesting that they meant to do much if they saw one. Guns stayed tucked into hip holsters.

The cat whose lane I had invaded decided to pinpoint me and started yowling again, which made one of the policeman glance over in my direction, making a mental note that there was a dark lane there but deciding against investigating it. Then a window opened in the building against which I crouched. There were voices using Thai, a man's and a woman's. These dead-looking buildings had caretakers, which meant that any further action on my part after the police had gone would at least have a couple of interested witnesses. I should have tried calling Ranya up from somewhere near the airport, but the risk of loitering in that area to search through a Bangkok phone book look-ing for the Ponchana's number had vetoed the idea.

The girl in floral pyjamas now seemed to be trying to persuade the policemen to do something, her voice going shrill. They had certainly arrived at great speed, which made this new phase of almost total passivity curious, and one of them began to shout back at the girl, this just at the moment when Ranya made her entrance from the wings.

The former Vice-President of my shipping company had always been what might be called a highly effective dresser, even her lateish morning arrivals at our Singapore offices turned into a small occasion when the rest of the staff were supposed to pause for half a minute to acknowledge the fact that she was once again with us, and to note what she was wearing. Obviously she still cared about the manner in which she came on stage, and the way she did this at past 2.0 a.m. on a steamy tropic morning almost at once quietened down both floral pyjamas and the shouting policeman. The two cops outside the grille turned to form part of the audience and the caretakers so near to my left ear damped down their running commentary on night vice in Bangkok.

Ranya had always been careful about her opening lines in any scene and, though I couldn't quite hear what she said this time and wouldn't have understood if I had, her few words appeared to completely resolve the situation to everyone's satisfaction. I saw something passing from her hand to a policeman's which looked like folded money. The policemen inside the grille bowed and the two men by the car laid their claim to the payola by also bowing. Ranya stood watching the withdrawal of the law, waiting through the banging of car doors, her body swaying slightly to give just a hint of feminine frailty, this movement setting up a glittering of silver threads woven through the purple silk of an ankle-length housecoat. Her slight bow towards the police car rather suggested a princess seeing lesser royalty off from the palace and the law departed on a noisy note from a rust-eroded exhaust. I took the only chance I was going to get that night and walked across the street towards the Ponchana. Behind me caretakers' talk flared up again. Ranya must have heard this. She stopped moving towards

a glass door, turning to stare out into the shadowed roadway from which I was emerging as a positive shape. Under
firm light I stopped. We stared at each other through the
grille.

I first saw Ranya Nivalahannanda at a Malaysian hill
resort not unlike the one from which I had just come. She
had been standing alone looking around at a roomful of
gamblers, her expression allowing out her contempt for the
lot of them, including their women. Then, as now, she had
stood very still, her head up, chandelier earrings glittering.
I remembered that I had thought she must be Javanese,
with a Hindu invader strain coming through strongly, to
which had been added a Dutch contact to account for eye
colour, but over a malt whisky she had told me that she
was pure Thai come south prospecting. I was beginning to
hope that I might personally become part of the prospect
when she had suddenly shown very clearly that she pre-
ferred a visiting Chinese celebrity to any hangover from
British colonialism. As a result of this I brought a slight
personal hurt to what was later to become our business
relationship. Maybe, staring at me, she was remembering
quite a lot, too.

'So it's you,' she said.

The floral pyjama girl had pulled the grille shut and was
about to lock it.

'Let me in, Ranya!'

'Are you on the run from something?'

'A plane for Europe. I was being exported by Batim
Salong. Remember him?'

'Naturally. That makes you a liability.'

'Just for tonight! I've some thinking to do.'

'Never what you were best at, Paul. Does anyone know
you were coming here?'

'The idea only hit me when my plane made an unscheduled stop.'

'I see. If it hadn't you'd just have been flying over me without a thought. And now you want to be the kind of guest who costs me money before he eats anything? Go back across the street and give those two at the window something.'

'What?'

'Tip them. They don't want trouble with me, but they'll expect to be paid to forget they saw you. Don't make it more than ten US dollars. Inflation is bad enough as it is.'

I went back across the street. Only one of the caretakers remained at the open window, a man. He took five dollars from me and shut the window. Floral pyjamas was waiting for me, somewhat nervously, in the still lit portico, but Ranya had disappeared. I smiled at the girl, getting no reaction. My smiles hadn't been working well recently.

Ranya lived over the shop. She said it was the wise thing to do these days, cutting out the risk of driving home to your luxury suburb with the takings in your handbag to find three masked men carrying guns emerging from the shrubbery by the front door. This way she had the security of a direct line to a police station which my visit had activated.

My hostess's creative flair was flamboyant. It had been given full rein in the conversion of what had once been the loft in the old warehouse that housed the Ponchana. She liked colour on herself and all around her and harmony was not involved, you were meant to be shocked into staying awake, and I felt that shock even though I was suddenly very tired.

I was given brandy and held my glass in a hand which just might have shaken a little if I had allowed it to. Ranya sat opposite in a chair with pink and yellow stripes. She told me she had been in bed, yesterday the restaurant had shut for cleaning, after which she always tried to take things easy. Without being asked, she said she lived alone except for the pyjama girl, who had a room and was training for possible management. I had the feeling Ranya was telling me about her life patterns because she thought it might be sedative for a man whose nerve had gone and who sat in one of her chairs looking around as though he just couldn't begin to take in the circumstance in which he now found himself. She didn't exactly stare at me, but I was decidedly under observation.

'All right,' I said. 'I know I'm older. Who the hell isn't?'

That seemed to switch off the homespun psycho-therapy. She smiled.

'You can tell me, Paul, that I haven't become one day older.'

So I said it, which made her laugh. Then she got up to give me more brandy. She certainly hadn't put on any weight, same figure, same ease of even the small movements of the body which are the Eastern gods' gift to so many of their women. Her hands, too, were something I always liked to watch, they put on their own separate act, and could talk when she wasn't. The second brandy on a somewhat empty stomach was making me sentimental.

'It's good to see you, Ranya.'

'Oh, is it? You could have seen me forever if you had wanted.'

'I'd have been your operative, not your husband. You know that bloody well. I wanted a rest.'

'Looks like that's just what you've been having, with Batim Salong chasing you out of Malaysia.' She paused, then added: 'I could have come with you to France.'

'We had this out, remember? After two months in Europe you'd have been bored stiff and wanting to open a restaurant in Menton. I've never thought Thai food all that good. And I don't think the French would like it much either.'

'So I was left just to buy back the Ponchana again?' she suggested sweetly.

'Ranya, you were wanting home to Bangkok long before I sold Hok Lin Shipping.'

She shrugged. 'Maybe. Now I don't like it here. The good days are finished. Shall we go back to Singapore, Paul?'

'No! If you've got a bed I want to go to that.'

'Sure I have a bed. Two. You choose.'

CHAPTER 16

There was a large assortment of multi-coloured pillows all around us. Ranya, with her elbow shoved into one of them, looked down at me.

'How are you feeling now?' she asked.

'Exhausted.'

'I'll get you some breakfast.'

'If you're counting on that to turn me macho, don't.'

'With you, Paul, I don't count on anything.'

She got up, but didn't bother about slipping into the housecoat, trailing it behind her from one hand as she walked towards the bathroom. I lay looking at a green ceiling, aware that I no longer felt lonely. It was nice. But I was still sure of one thing, how it would work out if we set up together, the basic principle of the relationship boiling down to rewards for good behaviour. If I did what she wanted for most of the week I could expect a really agreeable Saturday and Sunday, but if I didn't meet the standards set, *niet*. Soft and tender she might be at times, but you were never really allowed to forget the firm jaw. Also, Oriental women don't really believe in love, and I'm a romantic.

Breakfast when it came was mostly coffee with a gesture towards toast.

'You don't want anything with eggs,' she told me.

'Well, I do. I need building up.'

She didn't smile.

'Damn you! Well, all right.'

Ranya was a good cook when bullied into it. The omelette was sustaining. She was by then wearing shirt and slacks, one pink, the other blue. She sat on the bed to watch me eat.

'You should grow a beard, Paul. It might make your face interesting.'

'I don't want my face interesting. At the few parties I go to in France half the men wear beards to give themselves something to look after.'

'Who is your woman in France?'

'I haven't got one.'

'Liar!'

'Well, if you must know, she's enormously fat. Like a pumped-up airbed.'

Ranya giggled. That almost turned her back into the charming child she had once been up north in Chiengmai, the world's opium capital. She leaned forward to let her hands do the talking.

'You didn't bring a napkin,' I said. 'There's still egg on my mouth.'

'We share it.'

About 10.30 Ranya went to work downstairs. I rested for quite some time, then got up for the bathroom, a shower, and a shave with an electric razor thoughtfully provided for overnight guests. I then got into my drip-dried underpants and shirt and the bottom half of my KL bargain suit, managing to ignore a mirror that was determined to tell me that I had a hangover. When Ranya came upstairs again I was standing at a window looking down at a street flanked by offices that declined to have any exotic Oriental connections.

'You make second page,' my hostess said.

She didn't hold out a paper I couldn't read.

'What does it say?'

'That you're probably a lunatic. The idea is that the public must be protected from you.'

'You mean I'll be arrested?'

'Probably. There is a description of your suit. And they seem to have got your height right.'

'Great, isn't it? You can't get off a plane suddenly these days without the police after you.'

'Do you have a visa for Thailand?' Ranya asked gently.

'No.'

'That's what the police think, too. You'll probably only be in jail for a few months before you are deported. That is, if you haven't shot anyone in Malaysia. We have a new extradition treaty with down there. Paul, Batim is going to guess where you are.'

'You mean with you? Why should he?'

'He tried a few times to sleep with me.'

'So? You think he'll remember. You among the few hundreds?'

She smiled. 'The few hundreds said yes. I said no.'

'And he has never forgotten the insult?'

'It could be,' she said. 'And from what you told me last night you are not safe here. There is no place in this building you could hide.'

After half a minute thinking I said: 'If you have a back door I'll go out that way. Then all you have to do when the police come is say that I did turn up today wanting money. But that you more or less kicked me out in the street.'

'So, when I've kicked you out in the street, where are you going?'

'Back to Malaysia somehow. Maybe hitch-hike.'

'Don't be a fool. You must hide for a while until the

police don't care any more. That happens soon in Bangkok. In two days you are completely forgotten.'

'What do I do until that happens?'

'A friend will take you if I tell him to.'

'You have the kind of friends who will hide a man from the police?'

'This once, yes. He doesn't care. He is a prince. Very rich. Most Thai princes are not so rich. But Chundrapam's father was a banker. So Chundrapam is happy.'

'You mean he does no work? I take it he's beautiful?'

Ranya shook her head.

'No, ugly. He has a Cessna airplane. Sometimes I go with him. Down to Kra and such places. I like him. I don't like beautiful men. You are not beautiful. And never were.'

'Thanks.'

My departure to a safe house that afternoon was in no way dramatic. All I had to do was go down a stair to a small parking lot at the back of the restaurant where a Porsche was waiting. Ranya didn't come down the steps to make the introductions, and we didn't kiss. It seemed that royalty don't get out of their cars to greet their guests. I received a signal from a thumb to come around to the passenger door. I opened this and asked politely:

'Prince Chundrapam?'

'Sure. Get in.'

At one time Far Eastern bluebloods sent abroad to learn English almost always showed up for this splash of education at either Oxford or Cambridge. Japanese princes still do it, but the others now seem to look west to California or Hawaii, and from his extremely economical greeting to me I somehow guessed that Prince Chundrapam had chosen the pineapple islands. As Ranya had said, he was ugly, but with the kind of ugliness which suggests that it has been the result of planned breeding, as with pugs and bull terriers, a distinguished squashed-in look. He had small ears, very little nose, and rather wide-set eyes. He was wearing shorts, sandals at the end of bare legs, and a sweat shirt with the curious message 'Volcano' across his chest. His bare arms were well muscled, with strong-looking wrists. He got the Porsche moving rather too fast for the narrow streets, driving like a man who would rather be at the controls of a plane.

Ranya had been vague about this prince's status in the local aristocracy, and for all I knew he might be eighth or ninth in line for the occupancy of a seat upholstered in gold. In view of this I thought the correct thing to do would be wait for his conversational lead, so I just sat there, making no comments on the weather and more than a shade uneasy. I might have been a peasant picked up from the roadside by a Rolls with a crest on its door.

The traffic was bad through downtown Bangkok, with the temperature well up in the damp nineties. If the Porsche had air-conditioning this was dissipated by the driver's window down, which let in canal smells and exhaust fumes underlaid by strong hints about leaking sewage. My host's total silence while negotiating a chaos of lorries, carts and cars was understandable, but when we were out in the country and he could settle to a modest cruising speed of 80 on a bad road surface, the silence continued. I don't mind my own chat at all, but I get easily irritated by other people's, and after what I had been through recently no human noise was really very useful, just the sound of wind contesting the car's streamlining, with the engine murmuring that this speed was a joke and it didn't really settle in until about 120 m.p.h., which I hoped I wasn't going to experience.

It was flat country, no hint at all of the Burmese mountains which keep central Thailand from any access to the Indian Ocean, just rice paddy, lots of it, bored bullocks, and tall palms giving sun shelter to little clusters of wooden houses with uptilting gable ends to their thatched roofs. If anything, it was even hotter than in the city, little puffs of white cloud against a hard blue backdrop not promising to do anything about rain, or even a little shade.

A buzz from the dashboard was startling. The Prince reached out to pull a corded car phone from semi-concealment. He held the instrument to his head, only one hand lightly on the wheel, the speedometer registering eighty-four.

'Yup,' he said. Then: 'OK.'

I was handed the phone. The connection was hiccup-ing somewhat, but I recognized Ranya's voice without difficulty.

'Paul! There is something you must know! We've had a man in the restaurant asking questions. Not Thai, not Malay, Chinese.'

'So?'

I was getting the feel for verbal economy.

'The questions could have been from someone looking for you. I'm sure of it.'

'Ah.'

'Paul! Are you listening?'

'Yes.'

'Well, we don't get Chinese here. Not even tourists. Almost never.'

'It's that Thai cooking,' I said. 'How old was the man?'

'I didn't see him, but my waitress says he was quite young. She was surprised that anyone like that could afford the Ponchana. He could have been a student, she said. She's quite sure he wasn't a policeman.'

The hiccuping on the line had eased, almost as though someone had cut in to listen. There were restaurant noises, plates clicking, people talking too loud. I turned my head to the Prince, a hand over the mouthpiece.

'Can you tap a car phone?' I asked.

'Yup,' he said.

I took my hand from the mouthpiece. She said: 'What's the matter?'

'Ranya, dear, hang up!'

'What?'

'I said hang up! And don't call back!'

CHAPTER 17

Waiting for the police and others to lose interest in your case can be trying. I found this so in Prince Chundrapam's seaside residence. Strongly contributing to my unease was the residence itself. Where I live in France there is some very eccentric building, much of it hideous, a possible contributing factor to this being that Corbusier was French and therefore everything that he built, plus everything hinting at his genius inspiring other architects, is aesthetically bound to be OK.

The Prince's modest little palace was sub-sub-Corbusier, this mainly from its use of concrete in all its forms, roughcast and smooth, tinted and white, but mostly white. From the last bend in a private road through a patch of preserved jungle the house burst on consciousness like a loud shout. Also the sea beyond it didn't offer a bright tropic blue as toning contrast to all that white, the top end of the Gulf of Thailand carrying a lot of silt from assorted rivers which empty via the Bangkok delta, this turning the waters to about the shade of the drain-off from a large family wash.

However, the effect on me of the mini-palace from outside was nothing to my reaction to the inside. This was gloomy, except for one room, which was too bright. First there was the garage. We dipped down into this, automatic double doors opening to let us slide in alongside the inevitable

Mercedes that was presumably kept for use on state occasions. After the engine switch-off I got out in semi-darkness to the sound of lapping water. The place was also a marina housing a 25-foot cabin cruiser and a speedboat. I didn't ask where the Cessna was kept.

Going up into the house proper was somewhat like climbing those iron stairs up from a ferry cardeck to the plastic lounges where travellers are supposed to sit out the crossing, only these stairs were concrete. The door at the top opened into what could have been a ship's passageway, one long wall completely without any break, the other with doors at regular intervals. These gave access into accommodation of the type I would have expected to find if I had booked tourist economy on a Russian cruise ship. The cabins all had what is known in the hospitality trade as 'private facilities', which was comforting, but the furnishings were not, a bed, one chair, not padded, a sort of desk dressing-table with stool, and a cupboard. At first I thought my room might be the one kept for guests the Prince hoped wouldn't stay long but then, with wordless pride in what was clearly his own idea of the sweet life, he showed me four more along the corridor all exactly the same, including his own.

After I had made what I hoped had been happy-to-be-your-guest noises we went on to the living-room, this on the floor above. It was large and faced the sea, plate glass from floor to ceiling, with mirrors on the back wall pushing that not too exciting view at you from both sides. The decorator had loved two things, glass and white. You could see through all the table-tops as well as considerable portions of the chairs and sofas on which unpatterned white cushions looked too thin to offer much protection against ruthless angles and rectangles. There were no pictures and no flowers, but there was a bar which you could also see right through to what was on offer beyond. That was a lot.

Only two doors, also mirrors, broke up the back wall,

one into a small kitchen which looked like a condensed operating theatre, the other up another stair on to the roof, where it was revealed that the long blank wall of the bed-room corridor was one side of the largest housetop swimming pool I had ever seen. Its white-tiled bottom was marked with heavy black lines, presumably so that the Prince's athletically competitive guests would keep within their own lanes. There was a great deal of water in the pool, clean-looking, which meant that there had to be a filter somewhere if the sea was the supply source. I asked about this and got the longest speech yet from the Prince, this also involving me in being taken into a sort of control room and shown electrically operated pumps which sucked sea-water through a series of filters until it was fit to be swum in. When I wondered how often he changed the water, something that tends to worry me with swimming pools, he said every day when he was here. The emptying process took only about three minutes and, with the controls on the pipe reversed, it also served as a flush, sweeping away all sewage and household refuse. I was told that at low tide I would be able to see his pipe, which was wide-diametered, rustproof aluminium totally resistant to all forms of para-sitic marine life. Periodic disinfection of the whole system was automatic, presumably computer-controlled.

Lengthy explanations seemed to tire the Prince. He took me back down to the living-room and I didn't suggest that we waited for sundown before drinks. He didn't ask what I wanted, just held up a bottle of gin and another of whisky. I pointed to the whisky. He had gin. After a long silence, during which we both mostly looked at the sea, the Prince got up suddenly, left the room for about five minutes to return carrying what looked like an enormous Victorian family bible. He set this on a glass table in front of me and then, with his back to the view, quite solemnly turned over the top cover, this without a word of warning.

It was his life in photographs, page after page of them, the early ones clearly not taken by himself and not always in focus, the most interesting being of a boy of about six or seven wearing what must have been full court dress for a princeling. As compère of this show Chundrapam did not pull up a chair, continuing to stand, leaning over me, glass in hand. I was allowed a minute of staring at each double page before a turnover to the next, the timing careful, never hurried, as though in this bulky record of the years he had lived through there was absolutely nothing he was ashamed of. Schooldays weren't very interesting and by the time we had got to Hawaii I had to ask for another whisky, which was immediately provided. This section featured distant shots of surfers riding huge waves, one of whom might have been the Prince, and three very pretty girls of mixed racial backgrounds.

When we reached Ranya, as though he didn't want to have to talk about her, Chundrapam went off into his kitchen to get us a meal, leaving the door open. I was beginning to feel that my reactions to my host's life history had been inadequate, no comment on the Ranya pictures, none of which I liked, so I did some page turnovers myself and came to cars, calling out:

'I see you've had three Porsches?'

'Yup,' he answered.

There was no dining table. We ate off one of the low glass ones. I hate leaning forward from a low chair cramping my stomach as I put food into it, liable to indigestion as a result, and I got it. When we had finished eating the Prince introduced me to another of the things he lived for, which was hot jazz. He was a purist about this, for once turning his back on technological progress, sticking with the real thing, old seventy-eights, most of them needle worn. About 10.0 p.m. I felt it was time to go to my cabin, and he let me.

I didn't sleep well, conscious of my accommodation as confining. On a ship, with the movement, a small cabin would have been fine, but surrounded by cement it wasn't. I got that being in jail feeling, along with a sense of losing personal intitiative in a manner that was positively demoralizing. I couldn't remember, either, just how much I had told Ranya of what had been happening to me recently, lulled as I had been by that feeling of no longer being alone, plus her kind ministrations to various needs. What I *could* remember from Singapore days was how very much she loved action for its own sake, as easily stirred to the hunt as a she-panther who has caught a scent of antelope on the night wind.

I woke early, telling myself that I had never been asleep, the usual lie. On coming to bed I had found, neatly folded on the desk dressing-table, the kind of minimal swimming trunks which Olympic athletes and others wear to keep the world from having to do much guesswork as to what they look like naked. Underneath this flesh-coloured G-string was a blue and white short kimono. Since I had come with no luggage my host had thoughtfully provided me with the only outfit his male guests would be likely to need while in his house. I got into the briefs, with some tugging here and there, then put on the kimono, ready for the new day. I went down the corridor quietly, expecting to hear the kind of heavy snoring which tends to come from intensive gin-drinking, but there was no sound at all until I had passed through the living-room, where the curtains were still drawn. On the stairs to the roof I heard water noises.

No one who has drunk as much the night before should have been able, at that hour in the morning, to perform in water the way that Prince Chundrapam was doing. He was coming straight towards me, neatly inside a set of black lines at the bottom of the pool, using a crawl which caused a minimum of turbulence, all the power of arms and legs concentrated for thrust. It was beautiful to watch. I stood doing that as he made a racing turn at the deep end, a seal smoothness with practically inaudible air intake, with no indication that he had seen his audience. Then he was off again, still between those lines, towards the shallow end.

I removed the kimono thinking that after the performance just witnessed I should just hold my nose and jump in feet first. However, I did dive, hitting the water not too cleanly, surfacing to decide on the breast stroke which would allow progress with a certain dignity and no question of any rude challenge to my host. He stood at the shallow end waiting for me to come. It seemed to take a very long time before I reached a place where I could put my feet down and stand.

'Good morning,' I said.

'Hi. Sleep OK?'

'Yes, thanks. I mustn't interrupt your training. I'll just potter while you carry on.'

'OK.'

He was off. I did my backstroke, which isn't bad, and has the great advantage that when you begin to tire you can just fill your lungs and relax floating. However, I didn't do that, I kept at it, aware of the Prince passing me and then coming back from the shallow end, passing me again, going the way I was. He was doing the backstroke. I got out of the water to sit on a cement bench while my host did a couple more up and downs on his back to show me how it ought to be done. It was not gracious of him. When he finally came to sit beside me I said:

'You've done a lot of competitive swimming?'

'Sure. Never made Thai One. Just Thai Three. Too old now.'

I nearly said that I wished I'd seen his performance before alcohol intake had slowed him down. We went to breakfast. This was hearty and not Oriental, eggs, bacon, toast, all turned out by computer. After his third cup of coffee, which should have been the one helping him to see properly, the Prince said:

'Going to Bangkok. Back afternoon. No one will come. Cleaning women not today. Take anything from the deep freeze. Understand micro-oven?'

'No. My French housekeeper hates them.'

'Show you.'

That kitchen was intimidating. A huge deep freeze offered a choice for my lunch which suggested one of those menus that go on for four pages to let you know for certain that nothing served in the place will come to the table fresh. It was plain the Prince found me a slow learner, frowning as he tried to put over what I was to do with knobs and dials. He left about ten, wearing another sweatshirt, this model fashion-designed for inter-national athletes with little puffed sleeves set just below the shoulders, intended to show off splendid biceps. There was a new message in large letters across his chest. It said: 'University of South Dakota.'

I was up on the roof again by the time the Porsche went snorting down the drive towards that jungle screen doing duty for a high wall. He was right about no one coming. I never saw a soul all morning, even through binoculars, the paddyfields to the north apparently completely abandoned by the usual toilers in mud, and anything moving out at sea completely hidden by a heat haze which seemed to steam off the water. Once I heard a train hooting and thought I picked up the rumble of it gathering speed after it left the private station Chundrapam's banker grandfather had built to let him commute to Bangkok, but that could have been thunder. I had a sudden, acute attack of that alone-again feeling.

The house had no reading material of any kind that I could find, no books, no magazines, not even an old newspaper. There was a radio enmeshed in a vast music centre but all I could get out of it was Thai talk and Hong Kong offering Chinese opera for which I have no ear. My lunch, chosen because it seemed to be about the right size for one, was a pie which turned out to be made from those tropic fish which look exciting in an aquarium but when microwaved taste like unprocessed seaweed.

In the afternoon I used the pool, forcing myself to some training, three times up and back along the black lines and using the crawl I wouldn't let the Prince see. After that I pulled myself on to inflated rubber and just lay there. The sun was still hazed and there was a hint of a breeze coming off the sea which made everything very comfortable. I didn't try to think, just withdrew into the splendid emptiness of meditation, this with my eyes shut. A slight scraping noise made me open them. I even moved my head about but could see no hint of anything that needed to be explained, so I shut them again.

A clink of metal couldn't be ignored. Twenty feet away from my gently floating li-lo, at the deep end of the pool, was a man who shouldn't have been there. His shirt and trousers were standard tropic khaki but he was watching me through eyeholes in a black mask pulled down over head and neck. He held an automatic rifle loosely against his body. Then, in no hurry, he began to position the gun to fire at me.

I wondered if I'd hear the first shot. I heard it. Then another. Then a third. The man's rifle began to point down. It seemed to be slipping from his hands. He leaned forward as though to keep hold of it. He toppled into the water.

The splash made a lot of noise. The li-lo rocked. I looked from where the man had been towards the door at the top of stairs from the living-room. Prince Chundrapam had his Luger still held up in case he had to fire again.

My heart was hysterical, but I didn't make any sound. For seconds I couldn't produce a noise from my throat. I couldn't move, either. A voice in my mind told me that I ought to be paddling the li-lo to the side of the pool, but I wasn't able to. Chundrapam put the Luger down carefully on a stone bench, kicked off his shoes, and slid into the water feet first. I thought he was coming for me, but he wasn't, he swam underwater beneath the li-lo towards a stain that was spreading on the surface of the pool.

I went into the water, pushing the li-lo towards Chundra-pam who had surfaced with a body almost on his shoulders, a grim parody of a seaside rescue. We got the man on to the li-lo first, then shoved him up the ladder at the pool's deep end.

I was the one who pulled off the black mask. It was a young face, teeth showing in an almost rictus smile, as though he had been fighting death, not allowing it to hap-pen. I didn't at first recognize him. Then I knew. It was my room boy from Pindong, Chong Fi.

CHAPTER 18

'You know him?' the Prince asked.

'Yes.'

Chundrapam seemed incurious about how or where. He told me that I needed a drink, and I didn't argue. We went down into the living-room. While he was at the bar I said:

'Good timing.'

He looked up.

'What?'

'The way you arrived.'

He had no comment on that.

I asked: 'Were you just back from Bangkok? I didn't hear the car.'

'I don't go to Bangkok.'

'Then where were you?'

'Not far.'

'You mean guarding me? Did Ranya put you up to this?'

'I watch,' was all he said.

'After having locked me into this house. I could have got out through those sea doors to your marina if I'd wanted to.'

'I think not,' he told me.

He brought over the drinks. I stared at mine. The Prince stood at the glass wall looking out over the Gulf of Thailand, and after about five minutes took his glass back to the bar to do more than freshen it. It was coming on towards sunset, too much haze for this to become really sensational, the sea with a leaden look, unspeckled by any breeze. I thought about Chong Fi practically bounding into my room to welcome me to Pindong. The recently violently dead tend to provoke such memories. I got up to go to my room to put on some clothes, but turned at the door.

'When did you first spot the assassin?'

The Prince was lighting a cigarette. I hadn't seen him smoke before, it was bad for training.

'He was climbing the wall.'

I stared.

'You mean this *house* wall?'

'Yes. Chinese Tong training. To become spiders.'

I took a deep breath.

'I'm glad you realized that you had to come fast.'

He said nothing. I went down to my cell and shut the door. The shirt and underpants I had been obliged to wash myself were dry from the air-conditioning. I had a shower, trying not to think under it, but a silly idea sneaked in, that someone out to kill you shouldn't look as young as Chong

Fi. Or be as young. Killers should all have time-hardened faces.

I had just finished dressing when a rumbling started. It sounded almost like the noise you get as a preface to a big volcanic eruption, turbulence in the bowels of the earth before the eructation. I was aware of all that concrete about me and over my head, probably poured and not reinforced. I opened the door to the corridor. The noise was coming from the wall opposite, a pulsing interrupted by weird gurglings.

The Prince was emptying his swimming pool. Maybe he needed a good few laps up and down it in freshly sterilized sea-water before we both settled the business of what we were going to do about a body with three bullet holes in its back. I walked down the corridor accompanied by that roaring. The house didn't actually shake, but I felt it ought to. As I came into the living-room there was a sudden, complete silence. Through the huge windows I saw what I might have expected, out on the flat water an expanding circle of froth marked the outflow from the Prince's drain. I stood watching those rings on the sea slowly iron out and was still doing it when Chundrapam came down the stairs to the living-room.

'I see how your drain works,' I said, then turned. 'What do we do now? Phone the police? I don't like the idea of all that publicity.'

'We don't phone the police.'

'So it's taking the body out in your launch after dark? With weights on him?'

There was the hint of a smile on that pug face.

'We don't phone police,' he said.

'We've bloody well got to do something!'

'I have done.' He pointed. 'The man is out there.'

In dying light the grey, flat sea had ceased all hint of a disturbance from the outflow. The pipe was wide enough to take a body.

After a moment I said: 'I hope you know your currents around here?'

'Yes.'

'Where's he likely to end up? One of the tourist beaches down south?'

'After sharks?' the Prince wondered.

I had forgotten about sharks. He was watching me, the first real signs I had noticed of any curiosity about his guest. He used my name, it must have been for the first time, because I was surprised. I had been avoiding using his.

'Mr Harris, do you say prayer for man who would kill you?'

I thought about that.

'I don't know,' I said.

'I do not,' he told me.

Clearly a lapsed Buddhist. He ought to have been unhappy about killing a fly. Everyone seems to be lapsing these days. And the Thai princes were long the defenders of the true faith against encroaching Western imperialism.

He used the phone on the bar, three-quarters of a long room now between us, but I was still conscious of his continuing stare at me. The talk was in Thai, clearly to Ranya. She had always been a bad listener and at one point he shut her up with something like a sharp yap. That must have brought her to heel for she allowed him, without any suggestion of an interruption, quite a considerable flow of words that went on for a good two minutes before he put down the receiver on the bar counter. He signalled that I was to take over, then walked past me out of the room.

'Paul?'

'Yes, Ranya.'

'Are you OK now?'

'I think so.'

'He said you were not so good.'

'My knees stayed weak for a while. On that li-lo I felt

totally out of the action. And that it was for good this time.'

'Oh, poor Paul, I love you.'

'Don't let your imagination take over.'

'Pig!' She drew in a long, slow, very audible breath. I could imagine her breasts rising as part of the inhalation. Then she said: 'But we catch him!'

'That's right. You caught him. Thanks.'

'Paul, listen to me.'

I did that, as I always used to, even when she had gone on at considerable length. On this occasion she had quite a lot to say about how beautiful our relationship might have been if only I had been prepared to allow her the range within it she needed to express herself. I think she must have been paying expensive visits to a Bangkok shrink and had memorized the patter for use at moments like this when she was just about to push someone out of her door for the last time. I was getting the heave-ho before I had been given the chance to settle in, the basic reason for this, though his name wasn't mentioned, being that Prince Chundrapam was not by nature a sharer, something I suspected he had been making quite plain over the phone just moments earlier. Listening to Ranya, I found myself vividly recalling the stares I had been getting from the Prince even while he was talking to her.

'Paul, you don't say anything?'

'Like you told me, I've been listening.'

'All right. You listen some more. It's that woman.'

'What woman?'

'The woman at the hotel where you live at Kuantan. Josie you call her. What kind of a name is Josie?'

'It's a name I quite like.'

'Well, you don't like it when I tell you. See?'

'Ranya, what the hell are you getting at?'

'She is *bad* woman.'

There were quite a few things I could have said then,

one of them being an inquiry about the personal moral stance from which Ranya passed this judgement, but I went on just listening.

The main reason I had wanted Mrs Nivalahannanda as vice-president of my company was that she had been presented at birth with a natural gift which I could imagine her beginning to exploit by the age of eight months: charm which sheer intuition told her when it was in her interest to use and when not. It was totally easy to imagine her sitting up in her pram, if she had a pram, assessing the surrounding company and then beaming her baby chortles past gushing women to the man who mattered. If there wasn't a man who mattered available she would use the big switch-off and attendant females would explain to one another that the poor little thing was suffering from a bad attack of wind. The adult development of these rare talents had taken the form of absolutely no waste when it came to making the right contacts. In New York she could easily have become an Executive Vice-President of the Chase Manhattan Bank.

In Bangkok she ran a restaurant, but kept up old contacts. She had been on the phone to Hong Kong to use one of these, the topic under discussion being Josie, this a follow-up to probing questions asked me while I was under the influence of extreme fatigue. Ranya was now ready with a life story, which was certainly interesting, but I interrupted early on to cast doubts about the qualifications of the Hong Kong contact.

'Paul! Listen to me! I know this man for years. In Bangkok he comes always to my restaurant. In Singapore he is in our office. Maybe you meet him, but I don't tell you his name. When I phone him in one half day he phones back. See?'

'Right, Ranya, just carry on.'

Josie was one of those few hundred thousand Westerners

who have probably come bright-eyed to their new experience of the Far East but who haven't, in these parts, found
fame, fortune, or much glamour. If asked over the third
double gin most of them would probably admit that they
hated the area and wanted out, but couldn't get away.
Ranya made the slightly unpleasant suggestion that Josie
had almost certainly got into the air stewardess business by
having the right kind of body to pack into a tight-fit uniform, plus an easy smile to go with the kind of looks that
seem likely to stand up all right to two-day stopovers in
foreign parts when there isn't much to do but sit by a pool
and hit the bottle, that is if you're not into a short order
romance. Ranya then went on in this ungenerous vein to
say that perhaps Josie had been just sitting by a pool when
she got the offer of a much better job, this probably in Hong
Kong which was the sort of place where you got on best
flat on your back. Ranya then added:

'She has very good apartment. So who pays? She was
just stewardess.'

And not, apparently, on one of the major carriers, but
working for a newish line backed by Hong Kong finance
which flew mainly between Hong Kong, Calcutta, Bombay,
and South Africa, with periodic deviations to places like
Taipeh and Akyab.

Ranya had paused. I got the impression she was con-
sulting notes made during that phone call to her contact.

'So she is arrested, Paul. In Hong Kong. For smuggling.
She does this in many places, you understand?'

I understood. I was waiting then to hear that Josie had
been moving the leaf you can smoke like a cigarette, not
cocaine.

'Gold,' Ranya told me. 'For India. There is huge market.
From South Africa. Mostly to go for rich women. In that
country they are always hanging with gold.'

I had seen quite a bit of the metal hanging from Ranya

at various times. It seemed there was a considerable trade of smuggling into Hong Kong as well, the demand there being for the kind of trinkets the wives of potential emi- grants would wear through Customs. Josie had been caught making a delivery, and ultimately the airline had been closed down, a percentage of its employees arrested.

'What about the backers?' I asked.

'They fade,' Ranya said simply.

There was a pause and then she added, as if again from her notes:

'My friend says airline is Yellow Ox Tong money. So is hotel where girl gets new job after trial. You remember Yellow Ox, Paul?'

I remembered. I asked if Josie went to jail. The answer was for remand only, followed by a trial in which a cel- ebrated Hong Kong criminal lawyer had proved beyond a shadow of legal doubt that the lady, though obviously functioning as a courier, had done so in complete innocence of what she was carrying. Josie got a suspended sentence and that new job. She had moved into the hotel as under manageress. Ranya then summed things up:

'She is bad woman!'

After that the concern was for my immediate future. I would understand, of course, and I did, that it was necess- ary I return to Malaysia very quietly in order to leave it again at once on my returned passport and still operative visa. There was just no way that Ranya could use her influ- ence to sneak me back to Europe via Bangkok airport. There didn't seem to be any local warrant out for my arrest, but it still wouldn't be safe to assume that the police had given up the hunt for me. These days there was an increas- ing prejudice locally against foreigners who somehow managed to stray in the country. The Prince had agreed to fly me to Malaysia and once there I was to make my way to KL airport to catch the first flight out, no matter if this

landed me in Berlin or Budapest. I was to make contact
with no one in Malaysia before leaving.

It was quite like old times getting instructions from my
vice-president about what I was to do. I made no objection,
just listened, and this seemed suddenly to make her suspicious.

'Paul? You do what I say?'

'Haven't I always?'

'No!'

'Well, everything you've said makes perfect sense this
time. I certainly don't want to hang around in Malaysia.'

'You must not see Batim. You must not think you can
trust him.'

'I promise I won't do that. Ranya, I've been a bloody
nuisance to you, and I'm sorry.'

After a moment she said, her voice altered: 'It's all right,
Paul. Like old days. I got you out of troubles.'

'You certainly did. The moment I get home to France
I'll ring you.'

'Yes, please. Goodbye.'

She hung up. I was still at the bar when Prince Chundrapam came into the room. He had probably been listening
on an extension. He was wearing cream-coloured slacks,
and a matching shirt with no message on it. He went into
the kitchen without really looking at me. For supper he
offered a pinkish effervescent wine which had lost its
bubbles as a result of world travel, and was apparently all
for me since my host drank gin through the meal. The
computer gave us chicken which was quite good and vegetables smeared in a sauce before freezing, which weren't.
When we had eaten the Prince stood up to look down at a
guest still sipping his pink wine. He said:

'We go soon.'

'So it's night travel?'

'Sure.'

I didn't have any packing to do but I went to my room anyway and counted my money. There wasn't a great deal left, certainly not for a hire job in a Cessna. I wondered whether an offer to contribute towards costs in aviation spirit was in order or whether that would be a breach of Thai top echelon protocol. Back in the living-room I found him waiting, still in the same clothes but wearing laced-up boots and a leather waist belt with a holster from which projected the butt of a gun I respected, that portable hand cannon, a Luger.

CHAPTER 19

I don't mind small airplanes and once even tried to learn to fly one, but gave up on advice from my instructor who said that there appeared to be a communications deficiency between certain of my brain cells, which meant that if I went on with that particular learning process I would end up dead. He added the rider that if I really wanted to die that way he would continue taking my money, but he needed to be able to do this with a clear conscience. I got over the ego-bruising of the experience quite quickly, though I still remember enough from my training to want to give commercial pilots a few hints on the angle of take-off.

Prince Chundrapam's angle of take-off was all right, it was the course he selected after we were airborne which made me uneasy. I had been expecting that the pilot of a four-seater Cessna would base his navigation, especially at night, on coast-hugging from village lights to village lights, but the Prince wasn't having any of that, at first heading us straight out over the gulf as though our destination was going to be Cambodia. Then, at something like Longitude 105 he turned due south, and in a matter of minutes there was nothing but water beneath to both horizons, with not a light to be seen anywhere, not even from a ship. I sat trying not to think of the long swim if there was a sudden block in the fuel feed line, the Prince probably able to outpace the sharks with his backstroke, but not me. However, you have to die sometime as I always tell myself on all plane flights, and I managed to sit there looking, I hoped, in the dim lighting from the instrument panel, like someone who got his real kicks out of practically blind night-flying over water in small planes.

The moon wasn't much help, at first not around at all, and then when it did show up it was on the wane and hazed, really only serving to indicate just how big the Gulf of Thailand is, whatever it may look like on a map, and all the way down to Malaysia it gets wider. The Prince had a battered chart shoved down beside his seat and I pulled this over to look at where we were, asking after a moment of this what would be the first land we saw.

'Sungei Pattani lights,' he said.

I made that out to be at least four hundred miles.

'We should have brought sandwiches,' I told him.

The Prince kept staring ahead and, as if to make further pointless conversation impossible, he switched on his airborne stereophonic radio equipment which at once triumphed over engine noise to let us know that the sea might be empty but the airwaves weren't. He finally settled on what sounded like a boxing match from Saigon, this sport apparently once again permitted even under the cleansing Marxist regime. After about an hour of that Chundrapam reached out via dials for Hong Kong and got a soloist suffering from a strained larynx, none of her offerings at all soothing to my nerves. Then, almost as though our relationship had become intimate enough to be on the brink of psychic communication, the Prince reached down to the other side of his seat and produced a flask. He had a swig before passing it on to me. The content was brandy, which I found nourishing, but was surprised when the ex-athlete had another go at the flask when I handed it back, nearly bringing me to the point of asking whether drunken piloting was permissible in South-East Asia.

Before take-off I had been made to work, and quite hard too, filling five-gallon plastic containers with aviation spirit and stowing these all around the rear seating, indicating that wherever the Prince intended to land it wasn't going to be on an airfield where you just drove up to a pump. This seemed to indicate that my pilot meant to have a totally unrecorded flight, which suited me provided that we didn't land in some jungle clearing used by drug-smugglers carrying automatic rifles. I shouted my question about where we would be coming down over what had now become Oriental pop from Singapore. He shouted back:

'Kuala Krai. Near. You know?'

I knew it all right. The place had unpleasant memories for me.

'An old World War Two airfield?' I asked.

'Yup,' he yelled.

'I'd have thought it would be eaten up by jungle.'

'Not all.'

It was interesting that the Prince had experience of landing on a disused airfield in Northern Malaysia, but I didn't ask questions. It might be one of the picnic spots he brought Ranya to during their air outings. This and other speculations helped put in time until the lights of Sungei Pattani came up ahead, a cheering sight. I thought that surely we would now be coast-hugging down to Kota Bahru and beyond, but Chundrapam didn't do that, using the lights as a fix, then banking around to put the Cessna on course for Borneo, at least a thousand miles away. However, this turned out to be only a manoeuvre to approach the Malaysian coast from the sea over the island of Redang which I seemed to remember served as a beeline marker for his Kuala Krai destination.

After a flight across mountains which, in pale moonlight, looked cushioned with jungle, but which I knew weren't at all soft underneath, we started to come down, using the kind of landing lights which I don't think are fitted as standard on these planes, a sudden glare which showed concrete waiting in patches below, but none of it very flat-looking, slabs obviously worked on by secondary jungle growth for the better part of half a century, one or two of these practically upright. I sat in silence just about as relaxed as I can manage when the man in white has announced that he will have to use the dental drill after all.

When it was over I realized that I had been witness to the kind of landing that can only be produced by a pilot of genius. While it was happening I felt very near to yelping like a frightened puppy, consciously holding my teeth together and my lips outside them in a tight line. We hit, bounced, hit again, and then, in a white light reflected up all about us, didn't hit for a third time, but the Prince, with the wheels back on earth, had to steer his aircraft around objects that came up at us like slalom hazards. When we had stopped, and he was able to switch off engine, I couldn't quite believe it.

Finally I said: 'Well?'

He looked at me.

'Scared?' he asked.

'Very.'

That seemed to please him. He showed his beautiful teeth which I hadn't seen very often.

'Drink, Mr Harris?'

'Please.'

I got the flask again.

'Good planes,' he said, like a part-time salesman for the company who makes them. 'We get out.'

We did more than that, we got to work, still with the landing lights glaring, hauling out the plastic containers of air spirit which was then siphoned into the tank with a small pressure pump that didn't seem to be likely to be standard issue with these machines. It took twenty-five minutes before he was fuelled up again, ready for his flight back to a desirable seaside residence with a really effective drainage system.

While we worked I was conscious of the surrounding secondary jungle, youngish trees with climbing parasites already hanging on to them, both saying that if they were left alone for a few more decades they could most effectively wipe out all traces of man ever having been here. Shadows like the fat fingers of a fat hand seemed to be reaching out almost to touch us. The Prince wasn't noticing anything like that, but then he wasn't going to have to walk out through this stuff to get back to where people lived. Once there had been traces of a road into this field, and even some ruined huts, but it looked now as though all these had been smothered.

'OK,' said the Prince, putting the fuel tank cap back on.

We stowed the containers in the plane, after which I put a question showing concern for him as an alternative to the concern I was feeling for myself.

'How the hell are you going to get out of here?'

'Flares.'

'I'm not talking about light. Where's your straight run to get airborne?'

'I show you.'

We went out and set the flares. From what I could see, he was going to have to steer over cement that looked as though it had taken severe earthquake damage. If he crashed on take-off I could be faced with the problem of what to do about a wounded man on a disused airfield miles from human habitation. The Devil whispered that if I pushed off at once on my solo venture to get to the Kuala Krai-Kota Bahru road, but managed to persuade him to wait for daylight before trying to get airborne, then I wouldn't be around to see what happened. However, I told Satan to get behind me and made no suggestions. The Prince wouldn't have waited until dawn anyway.

Back at the plane I said: 'I'll need a flashlight.'

'Sure.'

'And your Luger.'

'No!'

'Look, this mayn't have grown into real jungle yet but all kinds of things that use the night will already be walking around in these secondaries. I'm going to need some protection.'

'You don't get my gun.'

'I'll pay for it. As well as for this trip. I can't do it now because I'm running short of cash. But I'll send Ranya a cheque from France. She'll settle up with you.'

In all that white light still sucking its sustenance from the plane's batteries he stared at me.

'Light fire here. You are safe. Wait for sunrise. You don't need gun.'

'Prince Chundrapam, almost certainly before I leave Malaysia I'll have need of your Luger.'

His stare continued.

'So? You will not do as Ranya says?'

'I'll leave this country soon. But not immediately. There's something I have to see to first.'

'That needs gun?'

'Possibly.'

'Listen, Mr Harris. You are fool if you stay. Even for one day more.'

'Perhaps.'

'I tell you something. It is not one man who comes to my house to kill you. There are two.'

'*What?*'

'Second man helps spider up wall. Understand?'

My breathing felt a little tight.

'What happened to the second man?'

He shook his head.

'I am running. I don't see.'

'Could he have seen you?'

'Maybe,' the Prince said.

If the second man was also a trainee of Mrs Kwing, he would certainly be able to tell the difference between shots from a Luger and automatic fire. And if there was no sound of automatic fire at all, just those Luger thumps, there was nothing left for the second man to do but get out of the area at speed to make his report back to command that it was Chong Fi who was dead, not me. Or he might have risked staying in the area to watch the Cessna take off with me in it, something to add to his news bulletin.

I would like to say that I took my decision to linger in Malaysia at once, but I didn't, I needed a good half-minute for it, and with the Prince staring at me all the time.

'I'll still need the Luger,' I told him.

He made an odd sound then, like a snort, which might have meant something to him, but didn't to me. He began to undo the buckle of his holster belt.

'I won't need that,' I said. 'Just the gun.'

'You carry in hand?' Then he smiled. 'Or paper bag?'

'The paper bag is a good idea. Could you find me one?'

'Sure.'

Probably left over from one of his picnics with Ranya. The Prince groped around in the back seat area for a carrier decorated with the announcement that it came from Bangkok's best supermarket. I put the gun into it and stood there like a shopper waiting for sluggish automatic doors to open.

'Flares,' the Prince ordered. 'Light now.'

Carrying my paper bag, I walked out to do the job. It took about ten minutes. When I got back to the plane he was already in it, looking down from the pilot's window with something like curiosity in his expression, as though for the first time since our meeting he was wondering slightly what made me tick. I couldn't really have given the answer to that.

The engine came on, prop turning, and the Prince shouted a sudden farewell that might have come from an old Hollywood film made back in the days when talkies were just coming in.

'So long, Mr Harris.'

I didn't shout anything back. He wouldn't have heard. I was certain that he wasn't going to get airborne. I watched him steer his craft, still on the ground, up to and then past the last of the flares. There was a switch-off of the plane's own landing lights. I couldn't believe it when I saw the red winking which said that he was clear of scrub growth and away, heading for Pulao Redang. He seemed to me to be going a lot higher than he needed to for his journey home, up to at least five thousand. Then I lost him, which left me with that lonely feeling again.

CHAPTER 20

Kelantan was once the most isolated and untroubled of the Malay States, with a right-angle of mountains to the west and south, the sea to the east, and a sizeable area of more or less impenetrable jungle protecting it from Thailand in the north. Kota Bahru, the capital, dozed quietly through the early decades of this century to a rude awakening when the Japanese chose it as the invasion point for their conquest of British Malaysia. Before I left South-East Asia there had been encouraging signs that the town was going to be able to go back to sleep again, but then contemporary progress built the east–west highway through the mountains and Kota Bahru had to sit up and keep its eyes open, bracing itself for tourism. There is an airfield now and an official classification of 'unspoiled', which means that if the mobs aren't there yet they soon will be.

On the road to Kota Bahru I got a lift in a Nissan truck coming back from a delivery of dried fish, with a Malay behind the wheel who had spent a sizeable portion of his cash sale on the palm toddy which his religion forbids him to drink. He was in a remoreseful mood, intensely introspective, and seeing a foreigner walking along the tarmac with a paper carrier dangling from one hand hadn't provoked any real curiosity, he just braked and let me in. I think he had been feeling the lack of the audience a good many of us need after having deliberately entered into sin. I wasn't asked where I came from, he just told me where *he* was going, his long-term future clouded by what he saw as the very real possibility of hell. Life was difficult, he told me.

He was a fisherman. He caught the fish and then matured them in the sun for some weeks, after which this raw product was delivered to others to be made into the *blachang* paste which is one of the gourmet features of the Malay cuisine that I don't miss in France. Staring glumly at the road ahead, he told me that anyone who goes to sea to catch fish has far too much time to think. His name was Emak, a married man with two children, but his wife was a lot younger, and he had a suspicion that she still had an eye for the boys of her own age group. He thought it a good thing that Islam was tightening up on what women could and could not do, and felt that a general return to a wearing of the yashmak was called for. What did I think about that? I said, after a moment's thought, that this face-screening device left the eyes exposed to the world to roll around in assorted directions. There was also the fact that a face packaged in that way could frequently be a lot more alluring than the same face unpackaged.

Emak considered that for two slow bends in the rattling Nissan, then told me that a cousin of his had nearly gone amok ten years ago. He had been on the brink of using a newly sharpened parang against the whole world when a sizeable group of his male relations sat on him, holding him down until the brainstorm had passed. Emak thought that his cousin was probably now too old to want to do it again, though you could never really be sure of this. I was asked if I had ever been near to going amok, which for some reason made me think about the Luger in that paper carrier.

'Once or twice,' I said.

Emak nodded, sombrely thoughtful.

'I know,' he told me. 'People look at you and think: That fellow could never go amok. But you *could*. What we should all do is trust in God and get on with our work. But it's not easy.'

'No,' I agreed.

Two bends further on he returned to the confessional.

'There's a woman I could go to,' he said. 'In Kota Bahru. Maybe my wife thinks I will. But I won't now.'

'Is that why you were on the arak last night?'

He considered that.

'I think so.'

In Kota Bahru we parted after a contact that was probably good for us both, Emak being most earnest about an invitation to come to his village only ten miles south of the capital to meet his wife and family. He said his wife quite liked meeting foreigners, it made a change for her. I said that after my business I might have to catch a plane south, but maybe another time. He said he would look forward to that, and gave me a most beautiful smile that might have come from a soul refreshed, then put the Nissan noisily into gear and drove off.

The only place that would give me breakfast in Kota Bahru was a dubious-looking Chinese restaurant where all they could offer was warmed-over noodles and something unpleasant done to last night's pork, but I was hungry and ate everything. While I was sipping green tea that could have been made from yesterday's salvaged leaves the proprietor came shuffling over with my bill. He was fat, wearing an apron stained with a week's cooking, unwelcoming on my arrival and staying that way for my departure. In spite of this I used my rusty Cantonese, asking where in town I could hire a car that could be left in Kuala Lumpur for collection. He had the kind of eyes that could be used for a good hard stare without any widening of the slits, and I had the feeling that he was doing that. He didn't answer for a good many seconds, deep thought bringing out perspiration on his forehead, then said abruptly that there was no such place, just local taxis. He said that none of them would consider travelling outside the State of Kelantan.

He was right, too. I spent nearly an hour looking for transport, the only offer coming from a man who hired out a motor-scooter on a deposit charge far exceeding its current market value. The idea was that I would recover some of this outrageous outlay when I had delivered his relic to his cousin who ran a shop just behind Kuala Lumpur's Batu Road. It was beginning to seem to me that the outside world had moved into Kelantan for a rape of its once-lovely innocence. That transaction, thinning down my wallet even further, was completed without a smile or an amiable word from either of the parties concerned. I put the Luger into a storage box behind the seat, filled up the tank, and started south.

Scooters have never been part of my experience, and it

took some time to get used to that one. The engine seemed
all right, given to unnerving bursts of speed which had the
machine wobbling, threatening me with the deep drainage
ditches along the road. When I was finally able to look
around instead of just steer, I noted that what had once
been semi-wilderness country was now showing signs of
being heavily affected by world population growth. Instead
of the occasional village under palms with thatched houses
up on poles and life-weary monkeys sitting at the ends of
chains, there were now villages, with garages in place of
the redundant simians.

Traffic wasn't heavy, a few cars passing at speeds the
scooter couldn't reach, but the trucks were worrying, the
drivers apparently all Emaks with their thoughts on other
things. I took corners carefully, never knowing what was
coming at me around them, twice narrowly escaping being
ditched. North of the town of Kuala Trengannu the road
seemed suddenly to tire of the sea coast, swinging determinedly inland, then south again through what was at first
secondary jungle but soon became the real thing, the road
a tunnel under the overhang from huge hardwoods. Where
patches of sunlight penetrated these had a green tinge, but
it was mostly cave gloom through which my machine put-
tered away at its all-out and slightly uncertain thirty-eight
miles an hour.

The tropic rainforest is a natural temple for the worship
of the Hindu she-goddess Kali, the many-armed, the giver
of life and the destroyer. The big-breasted lady is often
depicted with a naked man squeezed between the fingers of
one of her assorted hands, the man dripping blood. The
jungle has never seemed neutral to me, I see it as a place
where life is given and life is taken away, with nothing
offering any comfort in between. A day alone in that un-
relenting half dark, surrounded by the stench of new growth
coming and the old rotting away, is enough to undermine

the most carefully evolved philosophy of man's special place in the Universe. What surrounds you seems to demonstrate all too clearly that man hasn't got a special place, and never has had one. Exposed on my scooter, with attention not absorbed by any need for sweating physical action, that old feeling came back to hit me hard. I wanted the road to turn down to the sea again, to run once more just behind those long, glistening beaches where the centuries-enduring hard-woods with their parasite vines would give way to soft-branched casuarinas and palms.

Beyond a sharp bend there was a car coming towards me, a big Honda. It must have been doing sixty. The road was wide enough but the car was arrogant in its use of it, out in the middle, then over the middle, on my side. It came into one of those patches of light from a hole in the roof of leaves, a white spot dropped down, first on the bonnet, then the windscreen. Behind the windscreen and the steering-wheel was Mrs Kwing. I knew why she was travelling fast north on this road.

I had a choice, to drive myself into the deep drain ditch or be hurled into it by the Honda. If I was knocked out even for minutes that would be long enough for Mrs Kwing to put a bullet through my head. If I could stay conscious I had a chance of crawling to cover in the scrub above the ditch. I drove into it.

Impact seemed to shake my brain on its mountings, but I didn't pass out. I knew I had to crawl up. I was spitting out earth and sudden blood when I heard car brakes screeching. Then shouts. I dug in my fingers and pulled my body up, one foot firm on something, part of the scooter. I pushed with one leg. I couldn't feel anything in the other leg.

I looked down the road. It felt as though I was only seeing with one eye. Mrs Kwing was turning the car, risking other traffic swinging suddenly around the bend. Gears crashed. A rear door was open and flapping loose as the car jerked forward and back. Two people were on the tarmac, a man and a woman. The woman was blonde. The man was Chinese. He was holding a Browning heavy duty pistol, but not yet pointing it at me. Through the open driver's window Mrs Kwing shouted something. The man paid no attention. He was watching me. Then slowly, as if this was something from his own initiative, he began to lift the gun to aim.

There was a sapling bending forward under the weight of my body pulling on it. Still in shock, I had the lunatic feeling that if I could hide my head in those leaves just above I would be safe. It didn't matter about my body still exposed. My head had been accepted by the jungle wall when the Browning spoke. Without a silencer it is a noisy gun. The man seemed to be getting range by single shots, two, which nicked pieces out of the tarmac. I heard the ping from the second shot.

He seemed to think he had plenty of time. I realized I had stopped moving, my head safe. Panic then. I jerked, pulled. The next shots were not at the road, one, two, three. The sapling trembled. Leaves seemed to hiss. I got through the scrub wall as I heard feet running on the road, a voice I knew shouting. I rolled over thorns into a hollow, like a shallow grave. The hole wasn't safety, if the Browning sprayed the jungle wall a ricochet could find me. The huge hardwoods would bounce bullets. I had to get deeper into the forest. They could see where I had gone up the ditch slope. They would follow. Even in thick undergrowth I couldn't move fast enough.

I held that thought for seconds, and hadn't quite got rid of it when I heard the car again. The engine was revving as it came down the road in the direction I had been travelling. Mrs Kwing shouted, quite near:

'Gloria! Get in, you fool! Something's coming! Can't you hear it?'

I heard it. The rumbling was heavy from beyond the bend I had taken almost too fast for the scooter. In that jungle tunnel the noise reverberated. There was a slamming of car doors, then the sound of the Honda being bashed through the gears. It groaned past my scooter in the ditch. Unconsciousness I had somehow postponed claimed me.

I must have been out for twenty minutes, perhaps longer. I came round from the attention of ants, a whole platoon of the large red warriors biting my face. Maybe the blood attracted them. I sat up. A few of them fell off but others hung on. I had to use my hands and that hurt. Then, on my knees, I found that the leg which hadn't done much to help me up the ditch wall seemed to have become semi-operational again.

There was no sound from the road. The big truck hadn't stopped for a scooter lying in a drainage ditch. The machine probably looked as though it had been chucked there to rust away. I was pretty sure it wasn't going to be of any use to me now. This was confirmed when I got down to it, very slowly, using some parts of my body in the process very carefully.

I sat at the bottom of the ditch for my inspection. The scooter's front wheel was badly twisted, and that tyre flat. Fuel was leaking from a dented tank, the machine a write-off. I got up again, hoping that no parts of me were, and after a few slow-motion tests, with special emphasis on one leg, decided that I was a remarkably lucky survivor. I opened the box behind the saddle seat to take out the Luger which so far hadn't done me much good. It was still carefully wrapped in its paper carrier.

Sitting by the side of that jungle road waiting for help to reach me, I must have looked like the kind of hitch-hiker even the most humane of motorists would have accelerated away from, yet the big bus did stop. Perhaps I didn't give the driver much alternative, for I stood and moved out into the road, waving the arm that was functioning best. He could brake or kill me. He braked.

The bus was a luxury job, the kind that package deal tourists from the other side of the world expect to find waiting for them, tinted windows to keep out the tropic sun, tip-back seats, a loo at the rear for weak-bladdered geriatrics, piped musak, and possibly bar service even in an Islamic country. I was conscious of faces looking down at me, all made indistinct by the brown glass which kept them protected from any outside nastiness almost as effectively as the windows of a presidential limousine.

A door at the front opened. A young Malay in a peaked cap, which also advertised Malaysia Joy Tours, came down a step and stood staring at me. I thought that if I used Malay he might take me for some unfortunate native from whom his customers had to be protected, so I said in English:

'I've had an accident. I need a lift.'

There may have been just a hint of command nestling at the core of a polite statement, enough perhaps to keep him from backing up into his bus and slamming the door.

'You are wounded?' he suggested, also in English.

'A bit bruised,' I said, not realizing that about half my face was wearing a mud pack on a blood base. 'My scooter's a write-off,' I added. 'I'll just leave it.'

The tour guide turned to consult the driver, which put me at risk of having a humanitarian rescue vetoed, so I just assumed he wouldn't dare, and put my foot on the bottom step, swinging my body up into an air-conditioning which smelled faintly of disinfectant.

An American voice said: 'My God! What's this?'

The lady was in the second row of tip-back seats and staring. So were a lot of other faces all the way down the bus to the powder-room.

'I came around a corner too fast, madam,' I said.

'Oh! I *see*! You're *British*!'

That explained everything.

I sat down in one of the two empty seats just in front of her. The bus began to move fast, rising and falling on the kind of springing which suggests a bed in a honeymoon hotel. At the back I would soon have been sick. For the first time I became conscious of a heavy throbbing at one side of my head, this based back in the hair above my right ear.

The tour guide was staring at me again. He came forward to almost whisper: 'Kuala Trengannu is soon. There is doctor for you.'

'I don't need a doctor.'

'You must leave bus.'

I asked where they were going. He said to Kuantan. I said that would suit me fine. He shook his head. It was becoming a matter of money again, enough so that he could split with the driver. I moved to the seat by the window, pulling out the wallet which had survived my recent distresses, letting him see US dollars. We came to an arrangement which left me practically bankrupt. I stayed in the window seat, staring at the back of the driver's head. He must have been behind in his schedules, in a real hurry. A lot of the cornering didn't suit my physical condition.

Someone was suddenly sitting alongside. It was the lady from behind. She had taken off the dark glasses which had been giving her double protection against equatorial danger rays.

'If you go back to that john you can get water to wash your face,' she said. 'When you've done that I'll fix you up. I always carry first aid when I travel. I'm a nurse from Indianapolis.'

CHAPTER 21

Alone again, I walked down the track between neglected rubber trees towards the blue house which was the Li family fortress. While I was still on the Malaysia Joy bus there had been heavy rain, the jungle assaulted by it, the high tops of trees tossed, water bouncing off the road's surface and the drainage ditches turned into sudden streams. With visibility almost nil for a time, the driver had stopped his vehicle, screen wipers in a rattling frenzy and engine noise drowned out by what sounded like a waterfall hitting the coach's roof. Behind me the passengers had become uneasy, some voices of protest loud, as though this was the sort of happening which hadn't been mentioned in any of the brochures and against which they had paid a lot of money for protection.

I suppose my presence didn't help any, a threatening alien to their tour party even though the lady from Indianapolis had really tidied me up, with a dressing the size of a ham sandwich on one side of my head, this held on by something like a tennis-player's sweat-stopper. Then, as suddenly as it had started, the squall was over, the sun out, the jungle steaming its gratitude and the bus travelling at a comforting sixty. I was half-expecting a free issue of champagne all round to calm the travellers' nerves, but this didn't happen. When the bus stopped to let me off on a stretch of road flanked on one side by neglected rubber forest I think my departure probably had everyone feeling reassured that foreign travel was an OK thing if you were prepared to take the rough with the smooth. As part of her generous good wishes for my future the lady nurse from Indianapolis had said I needed three stitches in my head wound, and that soon.

The squall had left a lot of water still lying in pools on the red laterite of the track to the Li homestead. It had also left something else: much evidence of car tyres and, at one point, clear indications of a skid caused by a vehicle hitting an outsize puddle at speed, this almost certainly within the past hour. Even the slight exercise of a slow and careful walk from the main highway had set up a pounding in my head that could have been from an African talking drummer putting out an emergency message. I was also trying to tell myself that a considerable dizziness is not a threatening symptom, just something in the mind. I had been staring through the bars of the blue house's electronically controlled gateway for all of half a minute before I realized that the locking mechanism was not engaged and all I had to do was push. Security doors left open as an invitation to enter can be a little worrying, and the courtyard beyond had an almost purposely deserted look.

I stood listening. There wasn't a sound from anywhere. I went into the courtyard. In the middle of a paved area was an outsize flowerpot holding withered canna lilies. Weeds with the ambition to become bushes had seeded themselves in the cracks between flagstones. Parked by the outer wall, and as though left there to rust, was the old lady's tricycle.

In the Chinese tradition of making things difficult for marauding demons the front door was at right-angles to the barred gate. This was wooden, heavy, but also not locked, its hinges oiled against creaks. From the outer step I was conscious of the bulk of the mansion above me, its builders mean about windows, and some of these shuttered from the inside. I went into the gloom of the hall, waiting for sight to adjust, and again listening, hearing nothing, the stillness somehow laden with a smell that hadn't come in from the rubber forest, a reminiscence of recent meals and a hint of lingering people sweat.

There was Peke noise from somewhere above, one yap followed by a half-smothered grumble, as though someone was holding the dog's muzzle. I saw shadowed stairs straight ahead and, at the foot of them, in the right-hand wall, a single door. With the Luger held out in case it had to do the talking, I opened that door into an immense kitchen designed for preparing large feasts, this back in the days before sanitary inspectors. It had a cracked concrete floor, two central tables, one with a meat cleaver digging into it, a stone sink with a dripping tap, three built-in charcoal braziers and a modern two-oven electric cooker suggesting the start of an updating programme which had soon died of apathy. In here the smell said that the household cuisine was centered on garlic, even for breakfast. I had the feeling of being watched by luminous rats' eyes from mouldering cupboards, but this could have been because I was being touched by delirium.

What was interesting in that kitchen was no hint of any food preparation in spite of a smell proclaiming that there had recently been a lot of this. The tidy-up was complete, a kitchen blitzkrieg, nothing left out that might suggest cookery on a big scale, the clear-away betrayed by a stink that could only have been eliminated by an extractor fan. There was nothing in here to interest the Luger, no broom cupboard for the cook to hide in, no sous-chef crouched under one of the tables.

I went back into the hall. Opposite were more doors, but I was pretty sure these would be storerooms, rising damp in the rotting old house driving its occupants up at least one flight. I went up to join them. At the top of the stairs was a long, thin hall with windows at both ends, one of them shuttered. There was an open door to a room with its lights on. I could see myself in a mirror on a wall facing the top of the stairs, which proved something of a surprise. The man in there had hair fountaining up from a stained sweatband, suggesting the player who certainly isn't going to win Wimbledon this year and is about to take it out on the referee. That gun, held out in front up the last steps, made me look a lot more vicious than I felt. I didn't care for that invitation of light shining out from an open door, but I accepted it, the gun held just a little higher.

There was a moment when someone in there could have shot me, but only at the price of a hand cannon returning fire. No one wanted to shoot me, or at least was prepared to show it. What I saw was a tableau vivant so carefully arranged that a wide-angled lens could have got them all in one take, Grandma sitting on one of those black, hardwood chairs with which the Chinese disciplined their unfortunate bottoms for countless centuries, Mrs Li on a lower chair beside her, the lollipop daughter of the house holding a doll positioned to stare at me and the other little girl, perhaps a year older, keeping her eyes down on what looked like a Hong Kong comic paper. Grandmother's gaze suggested that she had kept her eyes fixed on the door frame for quite some time, waiting for my appearance. She had the Peke on her knee with its muzzle held shut, the dog's pop eyes sending out no recognition signals. After one quick glance up Mrs Li turned her attention down again to a piece of sewing on which she might have been working diligently for the past week.

I was beginning to get the feeling that there was no one left in this house likely to jump on me from behind a door. The general silence seemed without menace, more like surrender. In that stillness my armament seemed about as inappropriate as a handgun in a waxwork. I lowered it somewhat.

'When did they all leave?' I asked in Cantonese.

Mrs Li's needle, which had been shoved in and out of cloth, stopped. Granny went on staring at me. So did the little treasure sitting on the floor with her doll. Big sister

stayed interested in her funny paper, though I did get the
feeling that Mrs Li wanted to say something, a protest
maybe, possibly even a loud shout about what life had done
to her as a wife and mother, but she just couldn't lift up
her head to make a start. All she did was fold one hand
over the other. I again broke the awful silence.

'You won't mind if I have a look around?'

The Peke wanted to come with me as a guide, squirm-
ing and making gurgling noises, but Granny held him
tight. Still not really careless about the way I was handling the Luger, I moved out of the bright light and started
opening doors down the long, straight passage. The first
two rooms had shutters closed and an acute shortage of
necessary oxygen. Then one of them had a new smell in
spite of a slightly opened window. The furniture consisted
of a table and two small chairs, no bed, but when I
opened a cupboard the bedding fell out, eight sleeping-
bags which had been shoved in there, and with them
came an intensification of the smell. This was reminiscent
of the stink you get in a Youth Hostel dormitory the
morning after a previously very wet day in the Scottish
Highlands, except that the recent occupants of these
sleeping-bags had all been pork-eaters. Orientals like to
think that they don't have anything like the body odours
to be encountered in the West, but they have their own.
The Japanese still carry around the world that curious
olfactory identification that seems to come from straw
matting which should have been renewed the year before.

There were two other rooms with windows open which
suggested recent use, but no sleeping-bags. This didn't
make them innocent of occupation, a lady had left on the
floorboards three of the black hairpins so popular in China.
Out in the passage again I saw that the light was still
shining from the tableau room and the living picture could
still be holding, for I couldn't hear any sounds of movement

down there and Granny must still be frustrating the little dog.

One of the doors gave me a stair to the tower and I went up, flicking on a switch which lit two spaced 40-watt bulbs. It was quite a climb, the room in the turret having no door, its function as a communications centre very obvious, short wave radio, a cabinet serving as home base for CD, which meant that anyone up here could chat with handset holders out over a considerable area of what was flat country with the sea beyond. It would be most useful for chats with boats approaching the coast, or leaving it. I couldn't, however, see anything in this equipment suggesting advanced new technology, nothing that couldn't be explained away as the gear of an enthusiastic ham operator. I was pretty certain that Mrs Kwing had been the ham up here, though she hadn't left any hairpins.

I found that the power leads to everything in that turret had been cut, including the corded telephone. I didn't think a search for another functioning phone in the house would be rewarding. On my way down and out I did not revisit the tableau room, just gave a shout to say I was going so that they could unfreeze themselves. I expect they heard, though Granny must have gone on keeping the dog quiet.

I took her tricycle. I put the Luger in a jacket pocket, then slung the jacket over the handlebars. I hadn't ridden one of these machines since I was six and found the sensation curious, especially on a track with bumps and puddle hazards. The unstitched gash in my head put on a protest demonstration. I had to go fast, which soon had me pouring in sweat.

CHAPTER 22

Before the turning into the Pindong Hotel driveway I had to get off the tricycle to vomit in a ditch. When I straightened from that I felt much better, telling myself that all I needed was a little food. I got on my transport again but the smooth asphalt demanded a new control technique on a sharp down gradient and I kept my head lowered watching the front wheel while applying uncertain brakes. I looked up to a surprise.

The car park was totally empty except for a Malaysia Joy Tours' luxury bus with tinted windows which seemed very like the one that had quite recently given me a lift. As I came parallel a head popped up from the vehicle's offside and I recognized the driver who had gone fifty-fifty on my money with the tour guide. There were spatterings of black grease on his face and in that moment he was hating bus engines. We didn't greet each other, and I didn't pause for questions, the brakes wouldn't have allowed it. It was a minor miracle that Granny hadn't long since fallen off this machine and been killed.

As I approached the hotel's admin building and restaurant complex the nausea came back, but I hadn't time for another refreshing pause, just carried on, hearing from the beach the kind of shouting which meant that the bar down there had been open for business for quite some time. The cave reception area was empty, which suited me. There was no one behind the desk to object to my using the phone. I got through to the hotel in Kuantan which I remembered had advertised cruises in what had been my boat.

The receptionist put me on to the hotel manager. He was an angry man. Sixteen of his guests had registered for that

day's cruise, paid their money, and gone down to the dock
at the appointed time to find their boat had just sailed and
was already a few yards from the shore. The skipper had
refused to return to pick up the hotel people, megaphoning
that there had been a mistake, a double booking. He would,
he said, take the left-behinds the following day.

'That's no way to run a business,' the hotel manager
told me. 'We're trying to encourage tourism here. Who are
you?'

'Just someone wanting to go on a cruise,' I said.

'Well, I certainly don't recommend these people. We're
going to have to buy a boat of our own.'

I told him I thought that would be a good idea and
hung up. My call hadn't brought anyone out from behind a
curtain to see who was using the phone. I went up the stairs
to the admin section of the second floor, expecting to find
this empty, and it was, with the special kind of emptiness
you find after an evacuation of premises by people who
want to leave as few pointers as possible as to how they had
functioned in these rooms. There were filing cases left half
open, with nothing much in them. Mrs Kwing had taken
time to put a plastic cover over her typewriter and to pull
out the power plug, as though even when in a great hurry
she couldn't quite escape an instinctive need to keep everything neat. The office computer also had its plugs out, the
dead screen making a statement that the destruct signal
had been sent to its memory bank. Beyond the arch Josie's
desk was tidy, but it had always been, she was a put-
things-in-drawers girl.

I didn't open the drawers. The Luger made a muffled
clunking noise as I laid my jacket along the desk. I sat to
look out of the huge window. The bus people were clearly
enjoying all the surprise amenities of what I was sure was
an unscheduled stop from engine trouble. Two of the pedal
boats were out, and there were water-skiers, one of these

with white hair who had to be from the Malaysia Joy Tour. Just about the last thing this hotel needed at the moment was a terminal coronary staged by a non-resident who had suddenly cast aside all respect for his own advanced years. A slight sense of responsibility was starting to nudge me again, but I pushed it away.

There were footfalls on the stairs. I took the Luger out of my jacket pocket. The steps were in the hallway, then in Mrs Kwing's outer office, where they stopped. The gun was sitting in front of me on the desk when Josie came through the arch. She stared at me. I stared back. It seemed up to me to start the proceedings, so I did.

'Why didn't you go with them?' I asked. 'Or weren't you invited to join the escape party?'

She took a deep breath, let it out quite slowly, then said: 'I wasn't invited.'

'If you had been, would you have gone?'

She needed to think about that for a second or two.

'I don't know.'

'It'll be a good idea to tell your defence lawyer that you decided at this point to make a clean break with the Yellow Ox organization.'

'Thanks for the advice.'

'Did Mrs Kwing tell you I might be coming?'

'No. But I'd never before seen her look frightened.'

'Was she still here when the bus arrived?'

'Yes.'

Bloody fool that I was! I should have stayed with the bus tour! I asked if Mrs Chi Wok Tee was a Nordic blonde called Gloria.

'Nordic from a bottle,' Josie said. 'Will you please give me a cigarette from the pack in that right-hand drawer?'

I did that. I even struck the match. She had to bend over me for the light and could have reached out for the gun. Maybe she thought I would reach it faster.

She said, straightening: 'Someone ought to see to that head of yours.'

'There's a nurse on the joy tour.'

'I'm almost a nurse. I just failed the last round. A knack I have. Your room hasn't been touched. All your things are there.'

'It'll be nice to have a clean shirt and a change of underpants. You think I should just go over and lie down on that bed? And you bring the first aid box?'

'Why not?' A pause, then: 'Tell me something. Would you have shot Mrs Kwing?'

'Yes. If she'd resisted citizen's arrest.'

'You could kill a woman?'

'I've always believed in equality of the sexes.'

I stood, picked up the gun, then my jacket.

'You can give me the passkey,' I said. 'I must have lost the other one on my travels. I'll need half an hour before you arrive to play nurse. And I'll want some sandwiches. Don't put anything but mustard on the ham. You'll be sharing them with me.'

'The sandwiches will be beef. Why would I want to poison you?'

'I don't know. And I won't until we've had our long, long talk.'

'The passkey is downstairs,' she said.

We went down together. We weren't alone in the reception area, one of the tour party ladies came out of a convenience. There was just time for me to get the Luger tucked away. The lady had taken off sunglasses and, though her make-up might have been all right for the inside of a shaded bus, it was too much for the beach and had run in places. But she looked happy. Josie and I got a lovely smile.

'I think this hotel is real cute,' she said. 'I was just saying to George that I don't see why we shouldn't come back here and maybe stay a while. He's retired now, you see.

George made a lot of money in the boiler business and we just go where we feel like. He always groans when I start to heave him up and out, saying things like who's going to cut the grass when we're away? As if that mattered! I say let the grass grow even if it brings burglars. I'm getting terribly carefree, really. And George loves that bar down there right on the beach. Only when I came up here there wasn't anyone serving. Maybe that's something that should be seen to?'

'I'll see to it,' Josie said. Then to me, as if she had nothing on her mind beyond hotel housekeeping: 'It's Chong Fi's job really. You remember your room boy? He's been away for days. I don't know where.'

'I do. He won't be pouring any more drinks.'

There was no change in Josie's expression.

'Well, I'll get back now,' the lady told us.

When she had gone Josie stood waiting for me to round out my information.

'Dead,' I said.

She didn't ask how, just went behind the counter to get me the passkey, handing it over. I made for the door leading out on to one of the sanded paths and went down this towards the Orchid Suite. It was almost like coming home. Inside the pink was muted, all the blinds down. I opened them. The plants out in the sunroom looked as neutral as the jungle is supposed to be. The air had a dusty smell, as though there hadn't been much servicing going on here recently, the air-conditioning on economy. I turned it up, then went into the bathroom. I could have done with a long soak in the *ofuro* but there wasn't time for the water to heat up before Josie arrived with unpoisoned sandwiches, so I stripped and showered instead, taking great care not to get my head wet in the process.

I sat to dry off in one of the wicker chairs provided for the *ofuro* parties, thinking about my boat now well out to sea, and going fast. What had I left undone that I could have done? Alerted the Malaysian air force to bomb the escapees? Fat chance of any action there on the evidence I could offer, or from the police. The coastguard anti-drug-smuggling launches wouldn't be able to come anywhere near the speed of twin Gardiner engines in the job built to my specifications on the Clyde in Scotland. They could travel a long way on those outsize fuel tanks, to near Borneo if necessary, before they had to break radio silence to contact the friendly freighter which would take them north to Hong Kong. And once alongside that freighter they would scuttle the boat which had been built with love by craftsmen. It had once hurt me to sell it. A decent ending, perhaps, but from the wrong hands.

I came out of the *ofuro* room looking at that sexy bed, thinking how marvellous it would be if I could safely crawl into it to sleep for fifteen hours. I was pulling a sweatshirt over my head when there was a knock on the door at the end of the passage. I took the Luger and went down there, but didn't turn the key.

'Who is it?'

'Room service,' Josie said.

CHAPTER 23

I had left Batim Salong's jungle palace in a whispering Bentley and I came back to it in a not quite so silent self-drive Proton, the Malaysian national car. A surprise visit is not really an advisable approach to top echelon people even when they don't have royal connections, and back in those days when I had been in business with Batim he had always been a by-appointment-only Executive. I braked in a deserted courtyard but got out of the car to heavy barking

which didn't sound as though it came from a family pet. I
rang the bell.

The door was opened with surprising speed by the man
in white who had, not so long ago, stood on guard during
my interview with his master by the swimming pool. The
servant did not acknowledge my nod of recognition and he
wasn't the type of staff with whom you crack a joke as you
step over the threshold, but he allowed me in. I was put in
a kind of guardroom off the front hall; it was furnished in
a way positively guaranteed to keep the waiting visitor from
relaxing, hard chairs, and with one wall practically given
over to a massive portrait in oils of Batim Salong. For the
painting he had put on some kind of court dress and had
his hand on the hilt of a curved sword. The face glaring
down at me in no way hinted at the once-beautiful youth,
it was Batim the man in middle life, potent-looking, wearing
the authority that was his right both from heredity and
natural ability. There is a fine living to be made from this
kind of work provided the artist has learned the essential
trick of turning the sitter into a symbol of stability and
measured, sane progress.

It must be great to come into the office on a morning
when the bottom is fast dropping out of the market and to
be able to glance up at the wall on which is the you who
remains permanently unaffected by what the Index is
doing. When I was running Harris and Company down in
Singapore I never met up with a painter I could believe
would do me justice in this respect and, even if I had,
Ranya would have insisted that it was her portrait, not
mine, that was needed to keep up junior staff morale.

While Batim made up his mind whether or not to see me
at this time in the day, I sat under his portrait thinking
about the tactical mistakes I had made recently. There were
quite a few of these, the big one being that hanging around
in Kota Bahru for far too long and making myself far too

conspicuous in the process. A query from Mrs Kwing to her local agent would soon have given her the news that I had been in town and then had headed south on a scooter. The fuel capacity of a Cessna leaving Thailand for the south made Kelantan almost the only likely landing in Malaysia. The lady had come north to meet me along the one road to Kuantan.

The waiting-room door opened. It wasn't Batim's major-domo this time, just a younger clone wearing almost exactly the same house uniform. I was told in Malay to follow him. We went down a corridor towards what seemed to be an annexe to the play palace, the flooring underfoot beginning to give out those loud creaks just as they do in Japanese castles, the idea being to prevent anyone sneaking up on the Chief.

The room to which the servant opened the door after two unanswered knocks stated plainly that it was operations centre for activities which would not be under discussion in my company. I sensed rather than saw a whole wall of what had to be electronic equipment off to my left, but what I looked at was a large steel desk centred on an expanse of tiled flooring. Behind this sat Batim Salong. He wore an open necked silk shirt and what looked like a squashed-down mini-fez without a tassel at the back of his head. No sunglasses, even under strong overhead lighting, should have meant that even a flicker of warmth towards me would have been visible, but I didn't get a hint of this. Instead he just stared. I stared back. I could hear his breathing, as though these days he was becoming a candidate for the removal of nasal polyps.

He said: 'You get Mahmud killed. You are stupid. Sit down!'

There was a chair waiting to one side of the desk. I sat. He had turned his head slightly to continue staring at me.

'What's that attaché case for?' he asked. 'You look like a commercial traveller. Eh, Harris?'

Friendship was dying, if not dead. I had been Paul for years.

'This case holds the notes Mahmud was photographing when I jumped him.'

Batim straightened noticeably in his executive chair.

'When you did *what*?'

'Well, I got him completely by surprise. I wouldn't have survived a second round.'

'What happened in the first round?' Batim asked.

'A sort of accident. You could say he was incapacitated by it. Which gave me a chance for a serious talk with the man.'

'About what?'

'His future and mine. And yours too, really. In the end I was able to persuade him to become a double agent. He was to let me in on any information he was sending back to you. I made it quite plain that I would be paying him well.'

Batim had no comment. He reached out to a bowl of fruit, picking up a cold storage pear from Tasmania, which he inspected carefully for any signs of blemish, then bit into with a spurting of juice. While he was wiping his mouth and fingertips with a handkerchief matching his shirt I reached down for the attaché case, taking out of it a set of typed sheets clipped together and a small Sony tape-recorder. I put the sheets on the desk. Batim showed no interest.

I told him that I was sure he knew all about the disappearance of the management team from the Pindong Hotel, that is, with the exception of Miss Josie McCollom. I had thought it a good idea to get a statement from her before the police started asking questions, though the police hadn't, by the time I had left it, shown up at the hotel, which had seemed to me somewhat curious. The sheets now on Batim's desk were a signed and properly witnessed transcript of the statement by Miss McCollom which we were about to hear.

Batim took another bite from his pear, more careful about the juice this time. I switched on the recorder and after a moment's hissing Josie's voice began, perhaps a shade too loud even for that large office, but I didn't lower the sound. Batim dropped what was left of his pear into a waste-paper basket and set about lighting a cheroot. Josie's voice, even with the volume up, allowed out not even a hint of an apology for herself. There were no excuses, as bald a state-ment of a life lived as I have ever listened to. On this recording there were some condensations but no actual revisions on what she had said the first time round to me up in that Pindong Hotel office with its wide window over-looking the beach.

'I, Josephine McCollom, make this statement of my own free will and under no duress. I have been under manager at this hotel for some three years and nearly seven months. Prior to that I was employed for nearly a year as assistant manageress of the New Asia Grand Imperial Hotel in Kow-loon, Hong Kong. I secured this position after having been acquitted on a charge of being a member of a syndicate engaged in gold-smuggling out of South Africa. This was while I was serving as a stewardess on Asia Enterprise Airways based on Kai Tak airport. I had previously been a stewardess on a European airline but was made redun-dant, and had come to Hong Kong looking for work. After my arrest, with others, on the smuggling charge, bail was found for me by my employers, Asia Enterprise. They also provided and paid for my defence lawyer. All the others accused with me, except one, received jail sentences. I was acquitted. My lawyer had not been defending the others. I knew that he was costing a great deal of money. He proved, to the satisfaction of the court, that I had been the dupe of others in the gang. I do not believe that the airline for which I worked, or the Hong Kong hotel which employed me later, were in any way involved in the smuggling. In a place like Hong Kong practically everyone in business does favours for everyone else in business, so it is quite easy for the relatively innocent to become involved with outright criminals.

'I knew that I was being looked after. And when the trial was over I wanted the people who had started to look after me to go on doing that. I didn't ask questions about who they were or why they were doing what they did, they were keeping me safe. A woman in my position, in a place like Hong Kong, cannot be safe without protection. In my job at the New Asia Grand Imperial Hotel I think I did well. There were no complaints about me. I didn't live in the hotel, but had an apartment in a luxury block in Kowloon. I had a servant full time. I knew there would be a bill for all this, but I tried not to think about that and most of the time managed not to. I had a Chinese lover, but that wasn't part of the bill. I was sure of that then and I'm still sure of it. I began to see myself as the executive woman for whom a lover is part of the pattern, but not too important.

'Then the bill came. It didn't at first look as though it was that. I was offered a new job in Malaysia where I would be assistant to the manager of a hotel that was just opening. It seemed my run of luck was still holding. The pay was better than I was getting in Kowloon. There was a good chance that if I saved my money I might build up enough to let me get back to Europe. That was what I wanted more than anything.

'Then, at Pindong, there was Li. I loved him. I wanted to be part of what he was and did, whatever that might be. I had never really felt that way about a man before. I didn't ask questions. When I began to see things that secretly frightened me I trained myself to look away. Still the questions were there in my mind even though I didn't ask Li for answers. I'd been in that position before, working with the airline, seeing things that I knew had to be wrong but doing nothing about them. What I knew began to build up in my mind even while I went on trying to know nothing. I knew when the hotel cruise boat brought new guests for the blue house. We didn't do the cooking for them in the hotel kitchens, but we did supply the blue house through the hotel stores. Mrs Kwing was supposed to be housekeeper as well as secretary, and she did all the ordering, but I knew roughly what we were using in the hotel and what went out to the blue house.

'You're a fool when you are in love. It took me a long time to learn that. No questions to Li. He was so kind. That was what got me. Much more than making love. He was my protector. I didn't want ever to think about that other protector behind Li who had the power over both of us. I didn't know what those people were called in Hong Kong, just that they were there. And could do anything they liked with us. We had to obey.

'Li didn't just obey. He wasn't content to be a sort of manager. Those trips to Europe and what he was doing on them must have given him the feeling that he ought to be one of the directors. Perhaps he started by asking for more money. Enough to make his bosses in Hong Kong feel that he was becoming a nuisance. Even a threat. So they got him jailed on a charge that leads to hanging if you're convicted. Easy for them. No problem.

'That's what Li used to say all the time himself: "No problem." He used to say it with a big smile our guests thought was wonderful. And he gave the impression of being able to do anything. He even used to drive to KL airport to chase up guests' luggage that had got lost in transit. Things like that. No problem.

'Li wasn't into drugs. I would have known. There wasn't a mark on his body from a needle. He didn't take anything orally, I would have known that too. Maybe he did go on drugs in jail. Maybe he was supplied there through Chong Fi's visits. If you've been marked down for death and you are in jail you want to forget as often as you can. Li was much stronger than I am or ever will be, but I can see him doing that in jail. But he wouldn't run the stuff, he would never be a courier. His bosses wouldn't have wanted him to do that anyway, he had much more important work to do for them. I know that now. It's awful that he'll be tried for something he couldn't have done. I suppose I could be arrested as his assistant if they wanted to. I've heard the women's section of that jail is pretty horrible.

'I don't know whether this is a proper kind of statement that a lawyer can use, but I'll sign it.'

The tape whirred. I switched it off. Batim had been staring at the ceiling, as though not listening.

'The transcript on your desk is signed,' I said.

Batim lowered his head and his spare chin settled back around his jaw.

'How much of that was your work, Harris?'

'None of it. It's one of today's love-stories. With a rotten ending.'

The room's silence felt sealed in by the air-conditioning. Suddenly Batim's voice was loud:

'What do you want with me?'

'I want you to let Li out of jail.'

'I have no power to do such a thing.'

'Spare me that line. You could do it with a phone call.'

'No!'

'You know as well as I do that Li wasn't a drug-smuggler. There is no evidence that would convince any court.'

'The evidence of that case he was carrying is quite enough.'

'Not now. And not if Li gets a good defence lawyer. I'm going to see that he does. Batim, what do you want out of this? And why have you been taking your time?'

'What do you mean . . . taking my time?'

'You must have known very soon after it started up what was going on at Pindong, that the place was a staging-post on the Yellow Ox thug route to Europe. Which means a selection of Hong Kong criminals who see no future for themselves after the colony goes back to Mother China. They want out now to establish themselves in the West. New York, Paris, London. It would be my guess that the Mafia are keeping them out of Italy. Though I've heard that the Sydney police are already very worried. Must I go on?'

'Please do,' Batim said.

'All right. Those crooks can't get out of Hong Kong legally for one very good reason. You can't get a visa for anywhere to leave the place unless you have a certificate from the police that you have no criminal record. I'm told you can't buy those certificates at any price. So whole Tongs are emigrating without visas. With Yellow Ox operating one of the major routes. Perhaps almost a rest centre where the transients through Malaysia could lie up while their new identities were being arranged for them. They probably left this country quite openly with new passports, maybe even hitched on to one of those package deal holidays to the West. A man or two could just drop off the tour somewhere, say in Paris, without worrying the courier too much. Especially if the courier was on the Yellow Ox payroll.'

'Did you work all this out for yourself, Harris?'

'Not quite, no. I still have some useful contacts in the Far East. We keep up with cards at Christmas. Or the Chinese New Year.'

'It's the idea of those contacts which I don't much care for,' Batim said. 'And just what did you mean about me taking my time?'

'Isn't it obvious? I have great respect for the service which you would flatly deny that you operate from this room. You knew long ago that Pindong was a Yellow Ox operation. Yet you made no attempt to close the thing down. Why?'

'Perhaps we lacked the necessary evidence for such a procedure.'

'As if that would have stopped you. No, Batim, the answer I came up with was that you had done nothing because you really didn't mind too much what was happening so long as you had it all under observation. It could even be that you got a certain pleasure from the thought of all those Oriental criminals travelling, even via Malaysia, towards their new careers in the West. Provided, naturally, that you could make quite sure that not one of these emigrants had plans to settle here. I'm sure you've been seeing that didn't happen.'

'All most beautifully thought out, Harris.'

'Well, that's what I felt, too. Then I decided that, in view of our long friendship, ideas of this kind were somewhat disreputable. So I put them to one side.'

'How nice of you.'

He was looking at me from under drooping eyelids and I didn't care for that. When he spoke again his voice was almost soft.

'So you had other thoughts, Harris? Am I to hear what these were?'

'Sure. It suddenly seemed clear and very simple. You can do almost what you like in this country, Batim, but you can't do it in Europe. Maybe a cost factor comes into that, no money for agents over there. And I was in Europe. You weren't going to pull tight the drawstrings of this bag until you could be quite sure you had everyone you wanted in it.'

'I see. I wanted you in that bag?'

'You did. You thought I was a Yellow Ox operative at the European end.'

'Did I?'

'I can see why you were misled, Batim. For one thing, you find it hard to believe that I was really serious about leaving this part of the world for good. There had to be something more behind the move than just personal inclination. And you wondered why I had chosen France, a country with which I'd had no previous connections so far as you could discover. I suspect these questions were in your mind when you came personally to inspect my new set-up. Am I right?'

'No, you are not right. I take it that you are now telling me, Paul, that at no time have you had any dealings, direct or indirect, with Yellow Ox.'

His sudden use of my Christian name didn't mean anything, it was just a verbal lapse from a long-ago habit.

'I have never had any dealings with Yellow Ox, Batim. And you can just put that disreputable thought about me to one side. Making us quits.'

A moment later he said: 'Why did you accept a steadily increasing income from a company that was never at any time solvent?'

'Because I didn't know it wasn't solvent.'

'For a business man surely rather careless?'

'Perhaps. But I was retired. What do you want me to do about this statement from Miss McCollom.'

His voice was suddenly loud again: 'Take it away with you! I'm not interested!'

'I hope you'll be interested in Li. And make that phone call.'

'Get out of here, Harris. Now!'

If I didn't go one of the clone servants would come for me, maybe two. So I went.

CHAPTER 24

I was making a second search of what had been Mrs Kwing's bedroom, without real hope of finding anything, when Josie came to stand in the open doorway.

'I keep wondering about when the police are going to arrive,' she said.

I pulled a drawer right out of a chest and began to feel beyond the stop at the back.

'I told you not to worry about it.'

'Well, I can't stop worrying. Isn't there such a thing as guilt by association?'

'There may be,' I told her. 'But I don't think a prosecutor would like to build his case on it.'

'I can't understand why they didn't want to keep a copy of my statement.'

'Batim Salong is not officially connected with the police. And it wasn't something that he felt he wanted to pass on to them. Official files get awfully crowded these days. They have to look carefully at every piece of paper they add to them. Josie, will you stop brooding! I've told you, I'm sure you're in the clear.'

'I don't *feel* in the clear. And the under cook has just told me he's leaving. Moving his family out of the staff quarters today. He's got a job in Kuantan.'

'People in the catering trade are always moving.'

'I don't think it's just that. There are all kinds of rumours floating about. Mostly coming from the kitchens.'

'Then it's your job to put an end to them by a wonderful performance of everything absolutely normal.'

'The guests have got wind of something, too,' she said. 'Six of them are leaving before their bookings run out.'

'Maybe they've become aware of a loss of tone in our hospitality. But those bus people loved us, didn't they? Perhaps we shouldn't be snooty about taking block bookings. I can see that if you haven't got a class trade you really need the buses. And we haven't got a class trade.'

'I don't see how you can be so calm.'

'It's just an act, Josie. I've got boiling terror inside.'

'I've never really liked you,' she said, and left.

I gave up the hunt in Mrs Kwing's room as I had given it up in all the other places which just might have produced a scrap offering pointers to the manner in which this hotel had been operated. Since Yellow Ox had obviously been running Pindong for years it seemed reasonable to expect that some member of staff had got a little careless, just as they had always tended to do in the various organizations with which I have been connected. But there was not even a hint of such carelessness, which made it perfectly clear that Mrs Kwing's expeditionary force had been intensively trained in those getting out quick and leaving no traces behind procedures. Even the émigrés from Hong Kong must have been subject to alerts during their stays, rather like those stern lifeboat drills on the old-style British passenger liners. Probably there had been a set of lectures for new arrivals which included instructions to destroy by fire anything written, this including old cigarette packs carrying shopping lists. If it hadn't been for those lingering smells at the blue house, that kitchen hangover from big cookings, plus the more that slight stink from sleeping-bags, there wasn't a hint of what had been, for long enough, Pindong's real function.

I went over to the Orchid Suite which was as unwelcoming as usual, all that pink reminding me of other usage, which could have included assorted top people in the Yellow Ox crime syndicate, possibly even Mr and Mrs Che Wok Tee, almost certainly their travelling inspectors. I dropped down on a bed made for imitation love and brooded, just as Josie was doing.

I found I was suspicious of myself. Against normal instinct, not to mention natural prudence, I was becoming almost proprietorial about this awful hotel. In view of my money sunk in the place this was natural up to a point, but it didn't account for the fact that I was now frequently catching myself in the act of playing boss man. The question was: Why? Then, looking at a pink ceiling, I got my answer. It hit me with very near to a physical wallop, I had heart symptoms that might almost be pre-coronary. It could be that I did now own the Pindong Hotel.

I fought the idea. It was lunatic. This last string to Malaysia which I had hung on to to had been self-indulgent sentimentality. And after landing in the country my reactions had been sharply that the time had now come to cut that last string. I closed my eyes to experience one of those distressing periods when thought runs ahead of natural inclination, refusing the discipline of any control. Leading the runaways was a big query: What happens to ownership when the main parties involved with a piece of property suddenly evacuate themselves, leaving behind no forwarding address of any kind and just one man holding a packet of share certificates? Did those certificates give the one man the right simply to move in and lay claim to the whole property? I had no answer to this and was pretty sure that even a smart lawyer like Mr Ming wouldn't be able to come up with one at speed.

I certainly did not want the Pindong Hotel, but if I was going to get any of my invested money back I might have to establish my rights of ownership before the place could be sold off. Beyond that lay another runaway thought: Supposing I could substantiate my claim to this property, what sort of price could the new owner expect for a business which had been noticeably failing ever since the day it

opened? I needed a fresh mind as an assistant to my tiring
one. Ranya!

I couldn't use the phone in my room, the chalet lines out
were all through a switchboard behind reception, an
archaic arrangement which needed seeing to. I went down
the sandy path and into an empty foyer, with no one at the
desk and no one in the room behind it, though there was a
line out to exchange plugged in. I had to go through direc-
tory to get my Bangkok number and after that wait. Then
suddenly there were voices from drink taken, glasses clink-
ing, and crowded bar laughter. I could almost smell the
cigar smoke. It took a while to get Ranya who might well
have been by a table somewhere sorting out a little local
trouble between a financier and a tax inspector, this for a
ten per cent *pourboire* to her from both the contestants.

'Ranya Nivalahannanda,' she said with professional
sweetness.

'Paul here.'

'Ah. Hold the line. I'm taking this upstairs.'

It seemed suddenly very hot in the little office, though I
could hear the hum of the air-conditioning.

'Yes, Paul? You are not in France, I think?'

'No. Not yet.'

'And you are in trouble?'

'Well . . . yes.'

'Chundrapam told me. You took his gun.'

'I'm returning it by post. I've taken the bullets out.'

'You didn't shoot anybody?'

'No.'

'How wise. So you are not in jail?'

'Just worried.'

'Tell Ranya.'

So I told Ranya, at some length, the cost of the call
adding considerably to the debit column of the Pindong
liquidator's bankruptcy summing up. She did more listen-

ing than was usual with her and when I suggested she might like to take a note or two she said that was unnecessary because my call was going on tape.

I told her that I wanted her to use her influential friends again on my behalf, this time to find out whether, as I strongly suspected, the Hong Kong front for the Pindong operation had suddenly ceased operation, with no trace of staff or board of directors. I went on from that to what was really troubling me, did it seem likely to her that on the evidence I had given I was now an hotel owner? There was absolute silence on the line for quite some time, then her voice came again, this time gentle.

'Paul. I run it for you.'

'*What?*'

'Your hotel.'

'Thanks. But no! The moment the ownership business is cleared up, and if this place is mine, I'll sell it for the first offer.'

'If bankrupt there is no offer.'

'In that case I'll just leave it.'

'You pay taxes. Many expenses.'

'Stop this, Ranya! I just want that information from your very reliable sources. And phone it to me in France. I'm leaving for home.'

'But you must come back, Paul. So much business!'

'I'm damn well *not* coming back.'

'You want me to come down to see you? Easy. Chundrapam flies me to Kuantan.'

'Look, I don't want to mix it with Chundrapam. I've had enough trouble.'

'OK. You go to France. I phone you there.'

I said in a loud voice: 'Ranya! What are you thinking?'

'Nothing. I must go back to the restaurant. 'Bye for now. See you!'

She hung up. I went out into the foyer to sit in one of the

many chairs provided, all of them empty. The air-conditioning machine was chortling away, wasting money. The phone on the counter rang. There was no one but me to answer it. I got up and went over.

A voice I recognized said: 'Is that Pindong Hotel?'

'Yes.'

'Please, I wish to speak to Mr Paul Harris. He is in hotel?'

'Speaking.'

'Ah. Mr Harris. I have news.'

'Yes, Mr Ming?'

'Jail governor has phone to me. Mr Li is free from jail tomorrow. At midday.'

'Thank you,' I said, and hung up.

CHAPTER 25

All the way to Kuala Lumpur Josie kept talk going. This skimmed along the surface of a much deeper thought flow. Lengthy silences were not to be permitted, as dangerous. She had dressed very carefully, pale green linen with long sleeves. Her hat was even wider-brimmed than the one she wore for beach duty among the hotel guests, as though she needed that shelter not only from the sun, but to tone down heavy make-up.

The hire car didn't have air-conditioning so we had the windows down and on the whirling road up thousands of feet to The Gap and the whirling road down from it again, this kept us cool. There had been the sound of water, steep rocky streams refreshed by night showers, but when we reached the plain the heat pushed in at us, and the breeze made by the car's movement was smelly, like a dog's breath.

In the city Josie seemed to think that the noise of traffic was enough, and stopped talking. Her hands were in her lap, laid over her bag without actually holding it, and she kept looking down, as though worrying about whether she had used too bright a nail varnish.

I said, because I thought it was time I did again: 'You still don't have to go through with this.'

'I know that.'

'Josie, as I told you before we left the hotel, I don't really think you should.'

'I know that, too.'

This made me rougher than I meant to be.

'After that time in that jail and sitting in a cell thinking he'll never get out except in a cheap wooden box, he's not at all the man you knew.'

'I'm expecting that.'

'He was also on drugs supplied him,' I said. 'Probably the only way he could get any kind of rest.'

'All right! You don't need to go on at me.'

'I don't want to see you hurt.'

I did a bad gear change. The car jerked away on a green light.

'I have to know,' Josie said.

So I shut up and just drove, through traffic, past sky-scrapers which hadn't been there when I lived in this city, and which looked as though they still needed at least another half century to settle in properly. On high ground, well above the central open *padang*, was an apartment block built on the site of my old house, but I was too busy putting the car into the right lanes even to glance up.

The jail hadn't changed, an historic monument, high walls, and an entrance area turreted above the huge door in which was the hatch they pushed people through, both ways. At nearly noon there was no parking problem, and I pulled in alongside a drainage ditch almost deep enough to be a moat. We got out from the oven heat of the car into full sun heat that could almost have been a furnace holding on low. I produced my mopping-up handkerchief and Josie opened her bag to search for hers.

She looked up to ask: 'Where do you think we ought to stand?'

'I should think by the gates.'

'No. Not so close. Maybe over at that wall.'

So we went across the road to the wall, standing not quite opposite the hatch. Josie made a bid at showing she had perfect control.

'Have you ever waited for anyone else outside a jail?' she asked.

'No. Lucky, I suppose. Or my friends were. I've been locked up myself, though.'

'So you know how it feels?'

'I know how it felt for me.'

The car we had been expecting arrived. It was a hire job from Kuantan, professionally driven. In the rear seat, in a row, where they must have been overheating, sat Li's wife, his iced-lolly-sucking daughter, and Granny. The other child must have been left at home, possibly locked in a room at the blue house with the Peke. All three of the prisoner's relations fussed their way out on to the street side of the car when it was parked alongside the drainage ditch. Granny emerged last, still contriving to look neat in her black tunic and trousers. In her walk she hobbled just slightly, almost as though in youth she had experienced the bound feet of old China. The unbeautiful child started a whining about something, shushed by her mother, as though they were going in to a church service which had already started. Li's wife had abandoned her mother hubbards for a dress which must have been too tight for her even when she bought it. There were flower patterns, red and green, spreading like a contagion over white cotton.

She was wearing a hat which looked as if it had been lost for ages at the back of a dark cupboard. On the whole she looked like a Chinese matron who had, years ago, set out to semi-Westernize herself, but had long since given up the whole project.

It was Granny who was organizing everything, as I was certain she had been doing for a good many years now. She stood for a moment well out into the road, assessing the general situation and noting our position in terms of this. I was expecting her to lead her party firmly to a stance by the gate where they could grab Li the moment he was popped through the hatch, but this didn't happen. Instead the old lady ushered her charges in the direction she wanted, with some positively unkind prods into the back of the Li family's hope for the future who ought to have been a little boy. Granny seemed to be muttering as the three of them crossed the road towards the wall where Josie and I waited, and she shook her head once or twice as though trying to get rid of something buzzing around her ears. Where Li's wife and the child were to stand was pointed out, and the old lady then took up her position between them and us.

The whole thing could have been worked out with a compass. Both the reception parties for Li Fong Chi were equidistant from the jail gate across a broad roadway. There were some ten feet between the leader of her party and me, apparently appointed as leader of mine. The two leaders didn't look at each other, everyone now looking towards the jail entrance except little Li, who kept shuffling about and whining again. There were no iced lollies available, and she needed one. Maybe after a long drive she needed something else as well. Mrs Li tried to shush her daughter, but Granny simply ignored the irritation.

Out in front of us the asphalt shimmered. It might have been threatening to start bubbling if the temperature rose any higher. No cars came by and no pedestrians walked past as observers of our ritual. Josie had taken a pair of dark glasses out of her handbag, but almost at once put them back again, as though she had suddenly decided that she mustn't be wearing any kind of disguise. Her heavy make-up was suffering from damp stains.

I had looked at my watch just seconds before the hatch opened. It was twenty-five past noon. A warder came out first, his white shirt still smart-looking, as though he had been keeping cool in those cement passages behind him. He took a few paces into the road to look, first up it, then down, as though to make sure that there was nothing out here to frighten an ex-convict now leaving without a stain on his character.

After that came Li. If he was shoved from behind I didn't see who did that. Li didn't come out into the road, but stood by the hatch, almost leaning back on the studded boards of the main gate. The white-shirted warder had to push Li aside to get back into the jail, and in doing this said something to the man who was now a fellow citizen. Maybe it was a goodbye, to which Li at once replied with the kind of polite nod you learn inside to offer anyone in authority who may choose to speak to you. The warder disappeared, the hatch shut, leaving Li to stand looking across the road towards us.

It wasn't easy to guess which of the reception parties he was looking at. He was much better dressed than when I had last seen him, in a white suit that might have recently been drycleaned, the jacket over a white shirt with blue stripes, but no tie. Perhaps he wasn't wearing a tie because a warder had fancied it, and the disappearance of a necktie wasn't something he was going to complain about. Standing there, he looked like a man who isn't ever going to complain about anything again.

The Chinese can be explosively emotional on occasion,

but this didn't seem to be one of those times. There were no cries of welcome from Granny's party, the only real development being the youngest Li putting a stop to the whining. Beside me Josie was a statue, hands down at her sides, her bag hanging from one of them. She must have moved closer to me while I was looking at the gate, for the floppy brim of her hat now completely hid her face. It didn't seem up to me to do anything, like stepping forward and calling out a welcome to Li, so I did nothing, officer commanding a party offering no movement of any kind. Granny appeared to be under the same orders, these maybe coming from somewhere up in the sky.

The initiative was left to Li. When he took this it was very slowly, first a few steps out from a small, sheltering shade into the harsh sunlight, then a pause, turning his head as the warder had done to look both ways, almost as though searching for some excuse to stay where he was or even turn back to that hatch. There was no traffic coming or people walking in the road, he had to come on across it, out into the middle, where he stopped again. Then he looked from one reception party to the other, turning his head only slightly. It took a while, first the family team, then mine, then back to his family. I couldn't stand the silence any longer. I called out, and it was almost a shout:

'It's good to see you, Li!'

Silly thing to say. He might have thought so, too, but it earned me a turn of his head again. I hoped then that it was earning something for Josie, that he was looking at her past me. I don't know whether he did or not. What I was watching was his slow turn to Granny, then his steps towards her, not so slow any more, followed by his bow to the old queen who usually made her public appearances on a tricycle.

Granny said something to him in Cantonese which I didn't catch, and then she led her convoy past us towards the Kuantan hire car where the driver had been sitting in his oven watching through the windscreen. The pro-cessional was Granny first, Li next, Li's wife, and the whining child the rearguard. They all got into the car, Li up front with the driver. The car made a noisy start, a recently overheated engine almost at once beginning to complain. There would be plenty of joss-burning in the blue house soon, as prayer conveyance to what I was sure would be a big selection of deities with whom Granny had always kept in active touch.

'Come on,' I said to Josie.

She didn't say anything. We walked to the car. I opened doors. Even with the windows down you could have fried an egg on the plastic above the dashboard. Josie sat and found a cigarette in her bag. She lit it. The hand holding the match shook.

'We'll have lunch before we go back,' I said. 'And don't tell me you don't want any.'

'I won't tell you that. I'll eat my lunch. And I hope you'll buy me a drink before it.'

I switched on the engine and put the car in gear. We moved off.

'Josie, I told you not to come this morning.'

'And I said I had to know. Well, I know now.'

'That wasn't the Li you knew.'

'Near enough,' Josie said.

As we were coming into the town centre I asked: 'Are you still wanting to leave Pindong right away?'

'Tomorrow morning. When I've packed.'

'You don't have to rush things. I could guarantee your salary meantime. And I can make quite certain that the Li family won't bother you in any way.'

'What are you looking for, Paul? A caretaker?'

'I want a lot more than that. Someone to run the place while things are sorted out. And that could take a long time.'

'You're not tempting me,' Josie said. 'Why don't you bring Li back? After all, it used to be his hotel. Or that's what he told me. He could run it.'

'From the way he looks now I doubt it.'

Josie laughed, which was a surprise.

'I don't think the way he looks now will worry his old mother-in-law,' she said. 'They've got to eat. And there's no Yellow Ox any more to keep them going. She'll get him on the job.'

I thought about that and was still doing it when Josie asked: 'When do you go back to France?'

'As soon as possible. Where are you going?'

'Singapore. With all those hotels down there I'll get some kind of a job.'

'You hadn't thought about Europe?'

She tried the laugh again. It wasn't very convincing.

'Not with what I have in my bankbook,' she said.

We went into the hotel in which I had lost my passport because I didn't know where the good restaurants were these days. I had a long wait for Josie to come back from the powder-room while the ice in her whisky melted. She arrived expecting me to look at her eyes to see if they were red, but they weren't. They sell a kind of bleach these days to deal with that little problem, though I didn't think she had been using it. She sat down and reached out for her glass.

'Just what I need. You're looking thoughtful, Paul.'

'I've been wondering about what you said, getting Li back into the hotel. It would certainly mean I could leave quickly.'

'You want home in France, don't you?'

'It's the only thing I want.'

She smiled.

'Tell me about your villa.'

So I told her about it. We had another round of drinks.

They brought us the lunch menu in a padded folder and we both ordered steaks. After that Josie said:

'Well, go on about where you live.'

'There's a lot of wind. Everyone has meals in the open air. It's one of your duties to the place. Some days it's like eating out in a tornado.'

She laughed. It was a poor joke but her laugh was better than those earlier attempts. I thought about what it must feel like to be arriving in Singapore with a couple of suit-cases, no job, probably no friends, and no encouraging digits in your bankbook.

'Josie, I think you should try Europe now.'

'Well, I don't. Do you know any men down in Singapore who are looking for a girl with red hair and hostess training who can't swim in the daytime? I don't really mind what age group.'

'Not in Singapore. But plenty in France. Look, I have this first class open airticket. I'm going to trade it in this afternoon for economy. With my present financial prospects I'm going to have to get used to cheap travel.'

She was staring into her glass.

'And what are you going to do with the money you get back? Have a final booze-up at the airport?'

'No. I'm going to buy another economy ticket. For you.'

She smiled.

'Paul, you haven't taken nearly enough time to think about this. Supposing I liked that windy terrace so much there was just no way you could prise me off it?'

'I'll risk that.'

'Just because you've decided on the humane gesture of having Li back in the Pindong Hotel don't let generosity sweep you off your feet.'

'I won't. Are you coming?'

'Look, there's something you'd better know right now. I've always taken the easy way. And there have been a lot of easy ways. Some turned out all right. Some didn't. But they were always my choice. Never the difficult alternative. Get it?'

'Sure.'

A waiter arrived to say our table was ready. We stood up. At the door to the dining-room she stopped me with a hand on my arm.

'Paul, what I'm trying to tell you is that I'm a coward. I always have been.'

'We're all cowards,' I said. 'Let's eat.'